Out of the Depths

Modern Hebrew Classics
David Patterson, Series Editor

This is a new series that will present in English formative works of lasting significance that appeared in Hebrew during the fifty years between approximately 1889 and 1939. The series, edited by David Patterson, president of the Oxford Centre for Postgraduate Hebrew Studies, will acquaint the English reader with the quality of modern Hebrew writing in its period of renaissance. Future volumes will include Eliezer Ben-Yehuda's autobiographical *A Dream Realized*, translated by T. Muraoko, and *The World of Israel Weissbrem*, translated by A. Crown.

Out of the Depths

Joseph Chaim Brenner

TRANSLATED BY
David Patterson

WESTVIEW PRESS
BOULDER • SAN FRANCISCO • OXFORD

Modern Hebrew Classics

All rights reserved. No part of this publication may be reproduced or transmitted in any form or by any means, electronic or mechanical, including photocopy, recording, or any information storage and retrieval system, without permission in writing from the publisher.

Copyright © 1992 by Westview Press, Inc.

Published in 1992 in the United States of America by Westview Press, Inc., 5500 Central Avenue, Boulder, Colorado 80301-2847, and in the United Kingdom by Westview Press, 36 Lonsdale Road, Summertown, Oxford OX2 7EW

Library of Congress Cataloging-in-Publication Data
Brenner, Joseph Chaim, 1881–1921.
[Min ha-metsar. English]
Out of the depths / J. C. Brenner ; translated by David Patterson.
p. cm. — (Modern Hebrew classics)
Translation of: Min ha-metsar.
ISBN 0-8133-1427-5
I. Title. II. Series.
PJ5053.B7M5713 1992
892.4'35—dc20 91-39993
CIP

Printed and bound in the United States of America

⊚ The paper used in this publication meets the requirements of the American National Standard for Permanence of Paper for Printed Library Materials Z39.48-1984.

10 9 8 7 6 5 4 3 2 1

For Deborah, Louise, Daniel and Benjamin

Preface

THE HEBREW ORIGINAL of the story *Min ha-Meizar*—translated here as "Out of the Depths"—first appeared in the periodical *Ha-Olam*, Vienna, 1908–1909. It draws upon Brenner's experiences in his London period during the years 1905–1908, when he lived and worked in a printing house in the Jewish East End. As in most of Brenner's work there is a strong connection between his artistic creativity and real life. The story is concerned with a group of immigrants from Russia who work for a Jewish daily newspaper, and are caught up in a conflict with the owner which leads to an unsuccessful strike. The narration is fragmentary and episodic, but an underlying ethic of considerable force serves as a unifying factor. The general misery and poverty of the workers' lives are relieved by the moral values enshrouded in the personality and actions of the central character. As so often in Brenner's fictions, the message transcends the local and parochial background and assumes a universal tone.

Throughout Brenner's lifetime Hebrew was in a state of flux as writers struggled to give expression to the phenomena of modern life. Their search for vocabulary and the attempt to create idiomatic conversation using words and expressions which had not yet gained universal acceptance often result in a text which is difficult to understand. The problems are compounded by Brenner's literary techniques, which include stream of consciousness, fragmentation, shifting perspectives, emotive punctuation and the direct infusion of vocabulary from Yiddish, Russian, German and English with startling effect. He made a considerable contribution to Hebrew prose, not least because he portrayed society with shattering honesty.

This first English translation attempts to capture the flavor of Brenner's style while conforming to the demands of English idiom. The Hebrew months have been approximately equated with the English calendar for the reader's convenience at the cost of the overtones attached to the originals.

I am grateful to Joshua Knaz, Yoram Bronowski and my wife, Jose, who read the manuscript and offered valuable suggestions. This version is offered to the English-reading public with the sincere hope that it may convey something of the quality of Hebrew literature in the first decade of this century.

David Patterson
Oxford Centre for Postgraduate Hebrew Studies

Introduction

Joseph Chaim Brenner

Introduction:
Joseph Chaim Brenner

OF THE MAJOR CURRENTS in Jewish history throughout the last one hundred years, at least three can be traced to the wave of anti-Jewish violence in Russia which followed the assassination of Czar Alexander II in 1881. In the first place, many young Jews finally gave up all hope of achieving emancipation by peaceful means and threw their energies behind the revolutionary movements, in which many of them gained prominent positions. When the Bolsheviks seized power in 1917, the control of Jewish affairs was placed in the hands of Jewish revolutionaries, whose primary aim was to achieve total assimilation in an atheist society. It was largely due to their efforts that the social, cultural, religious and national hopes of Russian Jewry were effectively destroyed and that the Jews of Russia were denied any real contact with their fellow Jews abroad. Second, in the years between 1881 and 1914 almost two million Jews left Russia in search of greater freedom and opportunity in Western Europe and the Americas. The great majority found its way to the United States,

An earlier version of this introduction was published in *Jewish Book Annual* volume 38, 1980–81. I am grateful to the editor for permission to use it in this present volume.

thus gradually shifting the main center of Jewish activity from East to West. Third, a small but steady trickle of Jews made its way southwards to Palestine and began to establish agricultural settlements which formed the backbone of the new *Yishuv*, and paved the way for the creation of the State of Israel.

All three of these momentous events were reflected in the personal odyssey of Joseph Chaim Brenner. Brenner was born in 1881 in Novymlini, a little town in the south-east portion of the Russian Pale of Settlement, and was killed in Arab riots outside Jaffa in 1921. At the age of twenty-three he fled from Russia and lived in the East End of London for four years prior to settling in Palestine in 1909. During his own lifetime he was recognized as a major figure in modern Hebrew literature, and after a period of comparative neglect his reputation has grown steadily in recent years.

The originality of his writing is matched by a force of personality so striking that the impact which he exerted on his contemporaries is immediately understandable. For that reason it seems strange that the first English translation of any of Brenner's major works should have appeared only half a century after his death.[1] The reason may lie, perhaps in the fact that he was clearly so uncomfortable a person.

Clearsightedness is a rare and admirable quality, but the ability to see too clearly can be a disquieting gift. In Brenner's case, an insight bordering on the prophetic turned him into the conscience of his generation. His writings performed the function of a surgeon's knife, probing and incising his people's spiritual wounds, and ruthlessly gouging out the dead and rotting flesh. Unable by temperament to see the world through rose-colored spectacles and incapable of self-delusion,

---

1. *Breakdown and Bereavement*, translated by Hillel Halkin, Cornell University Press, 1971.

he portrayed life as he saw it—and what he saw was rarely attractive.

Yet the sheer starkness of portrayal proved therapeutic. Indeed, Brenner was an embodiment of the paradox that hope springs from despair, that optimism is born of pessimism, that all too frequently it is necessary to be cruel to be kind. His strength lay in an ascetic understanding that suffering and mortification cleanse and purify the spirit, that at times only the lash can restore the body to life, that an ice-cold shock may stimulate a nervous system which a creeping paralysis has rendered ineffective.

Short though it was, Brenner's lifetime spanned an age of agonizing transition for the Jewish people. His forty years were lived among a generation of the wilderness, for whom one epoch had inevitably closed but whose promise of salvation still awaited fulfillment. The pogroms which swept across Brenner's native Russia in the very year of his birth put an end once and for all to the hopes for equality and enfranchisement which had sustained Russian Jewry through the vicissitudes of its stormy history in the nineteenth century. Brenner grew up at a time when the lofty ideals of the movement of enlightenment, which had envisaged Russian Jewry splendidly integrated into wider Russian society, lay shattered and in ruins. The vast wave of emigration westwards was in full spate, and Brenner had every reason to flee from a life that had become intolerable.

Although raised in a strictly pious if poverty-stricken home, Brenner gradually lost his faith, and became estranged from religion and family. His own experience of the conflict between faith and reason is reflected throughout his writings, as his characters try to reconcile themselves to the harsh reality of a life without God. In his late teens he joined the Bund, the Jewish social-revolutionary party, and for a time edited its illegal Yiddish paper, *Der Kampf*. But disenchanted with doctrinaire Marxism, he transferred his allegiance to Zionist ideology, while remaining critical of its shortcomings. Nevertheless, the friendships he had formed among the Bundists were his salvation.

Drafted into the Russian Army, where he suffered acute hardship and humiliation, Brenner deserted (after two years' service) at the outbreak of the Russo-Japanese war. He was soon apprehended by the police and, as was standard practice in Russia, sent in convoy from prison to prison for identification in his home town. Fortunately, he was rescued in dramatic fashion by two members of the Bund at the risk of their own lives, and smuggled across the border into Germany.

Brenner later used his experiences in two works of unusual interest. The first entitled *One Year* is a detailed account of what it meant to be a Jew in the Tsarist army in the early years of this century. The second, *From Aleph to Mem*, describes the months he spent in Russian prisons after his desertion. Both documents contain a wealth of fascinating sociological material, and the penetrating insight and power of observation would more than justify translation. As in the case of so much of Brenner's writing, parochial experience is raised to the broader human plane, and the interplay of environment and character exerts a powerful appeal. The actual escape from Russia provided the material for a third, much shorter story entitled *Impressions of a Journey*, which conveys the tension and the terror of illegal border crossings, an experience shared by so many would-be emigrants at that time.

When Brenner arrived in London in 1904 his literary reputation had been established by a volume of short stories and a novel, *In Winter*, of considerable merit. Pervaded by an atmosphere of pessimism, pointlessness and ennui, the novel is concerned with the problem of the young intellectual who can find no possibility of fulfillment and relapses into despair. It had burst on the small circle of Hebrew readers like a bombshell and aroused a lively interest in its author. But during his first few months in London, Brenner chose to remain incognito, working for a pittance in the East End Russian Library, and later—after learning type- setting—as a compositor for a Yiddish paper.

The experience provided the raw material for one of his most powerful stories *Out of the Depths*, set in the East End of London and concerned with the tribulations of a group of workers on a Yiddish newspaper. The story contains much autobiographical material, and it is remarkable for the literary techniques employed for dramatic effect, as well as for the restrained passion in its depiction. The influence of Dostoyevsky is very clear. Brenner's use of irony is particularly effective in his treatment of the odious Shemaiah Taler and Hayyah-Rachel, his wife:

> Let me return to our theme: Taler's apartment. With the help of an English maid, the household is managed with great skill, if not with striking economy, by noisy little Hayyah-Rachel, the former Bundist, and even now an attractive woman, especially when, from time to time, she presents a popular talk at the workers' club. Admittedly, traces of her former life in the party may occasionally be recognized in the Hayyah-Rachel of today even in household matters; but essentially, she is already far-removed from all that! She has finally succumbed completely—I won't say to the family—but to the household! Only her laugh—a high-pitched, unnatural laugh, emitted through thin dry lips—reminds the walls of her apartment of her days gone by ... And within these walls I live too. And there are times when I reflect:
>
> What this household, just like any other needs to soften the damnable unpleasant coarseness is a healthy baby in a cradle—to soothe its crying, look after it, await its smile and its lovely dimpled laugh and surrender to its mystery. But Hayyah-Rachel, the "emancipated" Mrs. Taler is not a mother. Five

times a day she calmly consumes the delicacies and dainties prepared by the maid—and Shemaiah Taler is her mate. There's vision for you.

From the moment of his arrival Brenner conceived an intense dislike for the East End and the ghetto mentality which it bred. His contempt for the Jewish trade-unionists, for example, may be seen in *Out of the Depths* and in a short but powerful satire entitled *The First of May*. He loathed the ugliness and misery of his surroundings, and the life of degradation suffered by the newly arrived immigrants. Yet he made no attempt to come to terms with or even get to know English society beyond the confines of the East End; nor does he appear to have made a serious effort to acquire any real command of English. He never met Chaim Weizmann, and on the only occasion when he was induced reluctantly to visit Ahad Ha'am they scarcely exchanged a word. Indeed, throughout the visit Brenner sat with crossed legs, whistling casually through clenched teeth in what was clearly intended to be a most insulting manner. In spite of a common devotion to Hebrew, their views on Judaism and the Jewish problem were so diametrically opposed that neither could regard the other's opinions with anything but contempt.

Nevertheless Brenner's years in London were by no means barren. For almost two years, from 1906–7, he edited a Hebrew monthly, *The Awakener*, when the great Hebrew journals of Eastern Europe had ceased publication following the pogroms which swept across Russia after the failure of the revolution in 1905. Brenner poured his life's blood into his journal. He was publisher, editor, principal contributor (under a variety of pseudonyms), typesetter, printer, distributor and office-boy, while he subsidized the publication from his meagre wages as a compositor. But such was his passionate love of Hebrew that his iron resolve to keep it alive and maintain a circle of readers, however small, produced twenty-one issues of *The Awakener* in the face of seemingly insuperable obstacles.

In the first four issues of the journal's second year Brenner published his sole full-length drama, *From over the Borders*. Intending it to be his last and finest work, Brenner completed it in eleven days in a state of high emotional excitement. Locked in his mean and drably furnished room, Brenner worked day and night without even a pause for meals. Fearing for his health, a close friend finally forced his way inside and discovered Brenner striding up and down the room with his coat over his head, pausing every now and then to scribble, still standing, a few lines on the corner of his table, before resuming his endless pacing. Utterly absorbed in his writing, Brenner begged his friend to leave him alone until his task was done. A powerful play, it reflects its author's complete negation of diaspora life and ends with the dispersal of nearly all the main characters. It represents a scathing indictment of Jewish life in London's East End as Brenner had experienced it, and few aspects escape his censure. But the dramatic tension is considerable, and the author gets inside the skin of his characters in almost uncanny fashion.

From London, after one last, brief visit to Eastern Europe, Brenner made his way to Palestine, where he lived until his untimely and violent death. Arriving in the period of the Second Aliyah, or wave of immigration, he experienced all the trials and difficulties of those early years, including the dark and bitter period of the First World War. But whereas other writers have portrayed the romanticism and heroism of that pioneering epoch, Brenner depicted its stark, depressing aspects. The selfishness and lack of purpose which he exposed so mercilessly make the powerful and lasting nature of his influence all the more surprising. It is as though he galvanized society into action by rubbing salt into its wounds. Certainly, his ruthless depiction of all that was shallow and insincere in Palestinian society acted as a powerful catalyst on the minds of his younger contemporaries, and has continued to serve as a spiritual touchstone to the present day.

Apart from a number of powerful short stories, Brenner's experience in Palestine was distilled into two short novels, *Between the Waters* and *From Here and There* and what is perhaps his major work of fiction, *Breakdown and Bereavement*. All three are searing, uncompromising ferocious portraits of Jewish life in Palestine in the second decade of this century, and all of them make their point with a power of devastation that has few equals in modern Hebrew literature. But it is in *Breakdown and Bereavement* that Brenner's talent reached its height. A blend of penetrating insight, poignancy, honesty, compassion and artistry, the novel constitutes a human document of high order.

> If only everything weren't so dry and bitter and hard: the burning, sweat-sucking air, the filthy inn, the sickening, poisonous food, the alien cold surroundings; it was impossible not to dream of a comfortable place to live, a good meal, shade, a cool stream, tangled woods, tree-lined streets ... but in any case, it wasn't this that mattered most ... on the contrary: sometimes he would deliberately resist the slightest improvement in his life, refuse to escape the desolation, the apathy, the packed quarters, the filth, even for a moment. No, what never failed to crush him was the utter pointlessness of it all: it seemed monstrous to him to have to go on living like this, for no reason, as a Jewish "farm hand" always looking for work; monstrous when he found it to have to go out every morning and compete with a horde of strange Arabs; monstrous to have to fight all day long with the ill-mannered foreman; and then to return to the inn at evening and gulp down a sour, gassy gruel that boded ill for the stomach; and afterward to drop by the workers' club to yawn once or twice and read an old newspaper; and then back to the inn again, to a bachelor's sleep bitten into by all kinds of bugs; and once more

to rise with the ringing of the clock and work all day long until evening. And the work had no meaning, and the end was far, unclear, invisible, non-existent ... to go a year like that, two years, ten years, forever ... and never any change; no relief, no progress, no hope.[2]

In Brenner the writer and the teacher were inextricably united. He regarded literature as a social instrument—essentially purposive, and with an incisive and immediate impact. In spite of his early death, his output was formidable. Nine volumes of his writings—by no means all inclusive—together with two volumes of letters have been published, quite apart from his numerous translations and an impressive range of editorial activities. Yet most of his work bears a didactic stamp, and all of it stems from the actual and the present.

As an artist, Brenner lacks tranquility. His purpose was too urgent for any overriding resort to subtly integrated harmony and rhythm, even though his sense of artistry and form was of far higher order than has often been supposed. But the lack of polish is compensated by a certain rugged strength. Essentially a realist, Brenner was always preoccupied by the present, the here and now. Throughout his literary life his writings reflect the perception of his own immediate environment, to an extent which endows them all with a strong autobiographical flavor. But that perception was acute and deeply penetrating. With uncanny skill he laid his finger on the pulse of life, fearlessly exposing all its hypocrisy and cant, and tearing aside the veil from whatever he felt was sham and insincere.

By temperament incapable of moral compromise, Brenner saw the world sharply divided into good and evil. But the characters in his stories bear no resemblance to the black and white figures of the romantic novelists. He was not concerned

2. *Ibid.*, p.12 f.

with heroes and villains with all their facile predictability. Indeed, even in his early novels the principal character is a kind that was later to be called the "anti-hero." Brenner was wrestling rather with the vexed and complex problem of the effect of environment on disposition, and whether wretchedness is inherent in the human condition, or could it be alleviated by sustained and conscious effort.

This crucial question provides the key both to Brenner's pessimism and to the germ of optimism which it enshrouds. It is responsible, too, for the introspection of his characters, their constant questionings and painful searchings of the soul. In his earlier writings his interest is focused on Jewish life in the diaspora. For here Brenner was able to measure the interplay of character and environment against his own intimate and penetrating observation. Diaspora Jewry is examined, weighed and condemned as sadly wanting. It is judged to be compounded of hypocrisy and sham, a half-life, purposeless and ineffectual. Neither the traditional piety of eastern Europe nor the so-called enlightenment of the west could bear analysis—and Brenner turned his back on both. But condemnation is tempered with the plea of circumstance. Brenner could not tolerate what he found, but the evil might not be utterly without remedy. The iron had entered deeply into the people's soul, but there might still be time and a way to root it out.

National regeneration and individual responsibility constitute the central pillars of Brenner's message. The national home alone might offer a cure for Israel's spiritual and physical *malaise*. But what he found there held scant promise of fulfillment. It was not enough merely to transplant the characteristics of the diaspora to the soil of the homeland. A life grown rotten in dispersion became no less rotten by simple transference to the holy land. Hence the scathing uncompromising depiction. Only a conscious effort amounting to no less than a revolution of character could tip the scales in favor of regeneration.

Like A.D. Gordon, his fellow architect in the plan to rebuild the national life on sound foundations, Brenner postulated the basic principle of labor. Physical toil alone could redeem the individual, give him roots and a sense of belonging, and squeeze the poison of diaspora life out of the body politic. Manual work would remove the sickness from the Jewish spirit, cleanse it of its over-subtleties and emasculating introspection. But no less importantly, each individual was duty bound to scrutinize his conscience, and bow to his sense of moral responsibility regardless of the cost. Let every man come to an honest self-evaluation, and a clear understanding of the nature of his environment, so that he might recognize the realities of poverty as well as the uselessness of complaint. But let there at least be sympathy for the suffering and downtrodden. And above all, let no man tolerate injustice wherever it might appear and in whatever form. These were the principles which exerted so powerful an appeal. The appeal was all the more compelling once Brenner had died a martyr's death.

Brenner's novels are episodic and fragmented, a series of pictures that pin-point the significance of individual circumstances. His style is rugged, actual, almost colloquial, with the emphasis placed on directness of communication—hence the quasi-diary form of *Out of the Depths*. But the structure of his stories is carefully planned and he understood the secret of economy, an indication of the measure of his innate literary sense. Moreover, his ability to create atmosphere is masterly, a quality which endows even the briefest of his episodes with a startling air of authenticity.

Brenner's services to Hebrew literature, however, are not confined to his creative writings. His literary fame is based with equal firmness on his penetrating criticism. Widely read in many literatures, Brenner was by far the most European of contemporary Hebrew writers, and he applied the strictest criteria to literary appreciation. His efforts in fostering Hebrew writing were prodigious, and many a young Hebrew writer of his day, including Agnon, benefited from his sympathy and encouragement.

His impact on the growing labor movement, which was to shape the destiny of the new *Yishuv*, was striking. His strength of personality and absolute integrity impressed themselves upon the hearts and minds of a generation of idealistic youth. He preached a simple but powerful message—responsibility for everyone and at all times; and above all, compassion. It is a message still worthy of consideration.

Out of the Depths

Scroll Fragments

i

DECEMBER. HANUKAH.
It was in Maisey's kitchen that he came "shining at me."

"Shining at me" — What's come over you? ... Poetry at your age? ... Is that nice?

And especially since I still know nothing about him, nothing at all ... an odd fellow, solitary, out of the common run, not the kind you come across every day ... Yet can one rely on first impressions?

After all, I have only seen him twice, only twice altogether ...

On a foggy day, a real "pea-souper," the first day of Hanukah, in darkness at noon he first appeared to me ...

Appeared to me.

From the six million multitude of this great city *he* emerged, a stranger recently arrived; he opened the door and in he came.

A tall figure, strong, broad shoulders slightly hunched, firm, healthy features, swarthy ...

—A Hasmonean! ... Not of Jewish origin at all! ... the thought passed.

A few dozen other people sat around, Jews without doubt. They talked about seasonal unemployment, about exploitation, about emigration.

"There's a great difference"—Shalom Lieberman was explaining to some youth—"between emigration and immigration. Now listen: 'emigration'—means . . ." They talked, read the "Daily" I had brought in, argued unnecessarily out of habit, proving some point to one another, and eating bread and soup. He sat at a table in the corner for a while, then he got up and went across to Maisey, the owner of the "kitchen," and ordered himself a bowl of soup. The soup was made of millet, pale, and the bowl was small, but he ate a lot of bread.

He rose to his full great height—exposing a tattered hat and a patched top-coat, from under which he extracted three farthings to pay for the soup, and eight for the lumps of bread—and then sat down again leaning on the table.

The gloom gathered and thickened. It was two o'clock in the afternoon. The gas was lit—and still he sat on, silent, his open face weary.

I don't know . . . I am wary of imagination . . . but such, it seems to me, was the truth, the *truth*.

As the sudden smiling glow of gaslight in the floating mists fell on his full, generous features, its rays about his face and on the black, reddish hair of his tousled beard with its curling tip—there flashed across my mind a memory of daybreak in my native land, my native sun, in the book of my first childhood—my "bible" . . .

That was four days ago. I saw him again yesterday, when I was standing at my corner—and he passed by . . .

ii

The tenth of January.

Yes, indeed, the tenth of January . . . From the ninth of

August to the tenth of January ... more than five months have passed, then, since the day I arrived here. Wonderful!

More than five months. A whole epoch. A whole epoch—and what does it amount to?

What does it amount to? ... Throughout all this time I have lived by selling Jewish papers, especially "The Daily Crab." I am at it all day and half the night. I live with poor Shalom Lieberman in the meeting room of the "International Association of Typesetters in London," in the apartment of its president, the journalist Shemaiah Taler; and I feed off the board of that well-known hotelier Maisey. Sometimes I visit fellow exiles in the adjoining houses, and witness chronic poverty, chronic; no bread, no money to pay the doctor—anguish, anguish, unwanted anguish, liquid anguish, poured out ceaselessly and without hope ... A crying shame! ... But there I'm off again ...

No, no. I'll stop that. I am twenty five years old. I have taken myself into exile and come to a Jewish ghetto in a European capital ... yes, yes ... European. So what now? I am a stranger to the current speech, a stranger to the gentile population of the land, and far removed from my fellow Israelites, whose newspapers I sell them. Stripped of any material framework, of any trace of congenial company, of any spiritual satisfaction; tired and weary from a past of "Heders" and "Yeshivas," peripheral studenthood, a life of "organizations," prisons, military service, pogroms. And none of it sustains me, it gives me no fulfillment. In my free hours and my days off from selling papers there is nothing to do and nowhere to escape the heavy, silent, relentless boredom. If I could only find relief from this nagging stomach ailment, which began some time ago and keeps recurring, gnawing and gnawing my flesh like a worm ...

But no, no, no! God forbid! I don't, I really don't want to write of this! There is no need to write of this, no need at all!

So wipe the yawn off your mouth, and the awful look of disinterest from your eye. I won't go on torturing myself with a pointless old dirge that has become nauseating. True, true. It is an old dirge, and yet the one, the only one our hearts are full of, the only story we relate and listen to, the only tale with only one ending, the same ending which all tales have, even the most interesting. It is this life, this and no other, which is of necessity my own life and the life of all my contemporaries, both those who have been uprooted and those who stayed where they were. No use obscuring the fact with highfalutin talk, no matter how interesting and highfalutin it is: about strength of spirit and freedom of flesh, heroic action and revolutionary deed. Let them sing of houses full of remedies for dire ills and tinkling pianos, of the exploitation of the poor or of aesthetic longings. But I'm talking about unnecessary things! I can't get it out.

Never mind, whichever way it is: they are right, quite right. There is no point in superfluous repetition of the obvious, the prevalence of poverty and pain, even *sotto voce*. For my voice is certainly muted, muted. But that is not the way. Not with sighs, not with shakings of the head, not with pitiful tales. Vision! Vision!

iii

Yes, vision, vision . . .

Vision! . . . But where is vision to be found? Where can I find vision?

Where can I find vision, when I lodge in Shemaiah Taler's apartment together with Shalom Lieberman?

Not so fast! Who is this Shemaiah Taler? Who is Shalom Lieberman?

* * *

Shalom Lieberman is a typesetter, who works in the printing press of "The Daily Crab," the paper from which I, too, derive my livelihood by selling two or three dozen copies every day. The latter—I mean my neighbor Lieberman, not the daily paper, nor even the lord and master Mr. Crab who owns it, about all of which more may be said perhaps in greater detail at a later stage in my quest for "vision"—is a delicate young fellow of a little less than twenty with a sandy mop of hair, a face like a grasshopper, and attractive pale blue, shining watery eyes, who, like myself, had left Russia not long previously. Three of his top front teeth are missing, and the rest are small, partly decayed and as yellow as his hair. Yet even this disfigurement—along with the poor and worn out clothes he always wears—seems to lend his appearance a kind of warmth, a certain approach to people. Indeed—this is the man of "vision" speaking—there are many fine lads in the ranks of our people, the chosen people; there are many fine lads among our young workers, whose like you will never find among any other people in such surroundings! But Lieberman is also something of a scholar, who can set all kinds of manuscripts, and he regularly complains to me as follows:

Just listen to this! Isn't it marvelous! Many people imagine that typesetters as a class are not so boorish and ignorant as other workers. It's a mistake, a fundamental mistake. I doubt whether any of the other workers' unions contain so many boors and ignoramuses as ours. It's frightening, frightening! I'm the secretary of our union, you know, in an honorary capacity of course, and I understand what I'm talking about. Vulgar people—a frightening mob! And as a class—common, empty, with no redeeming features. I've already remarked on it more than once to our president, Taler. What's the point—I say to him—in having meetings without content. We ought to arrange proper lessons for them in sociology, physiology, history and the like. And another thing: because the meetings have so little content, the members are reluctant to come. Now if there was something to learn at the meeting, they would be glad to come. It's my belief that every man wants to learn something. Ask them—I say to Taler—even about our own work, its history, all the different branches, and they won't be able to answer at all. They don't know the first thing about it. I believe they wouldn't even know who invented the science of printing, who Gutenberg was and when he lived! Isn't it marvelous? That's what I argue to Taler. But go and talk to the wall ... (with a deep sigh) you know Taler ...

I do indeed know Taler, the head of the "International Association of Typesetters in London," in whose apartment (in the Association's meeting room) I live together with Lieberman. Taler is a Europeanized Jewish gentleman in the prime of life, with a clever-sounding voice, a voice heavy with intonation and emphasis, a deliberate, resonant voice. He had arrived in London some years prior to the revolution (the Russian one, of course, not the London one), and even then he was a sceptic, a carper, a pessimist, an unbeliever, a scoffer, a "heretic on principle"—deep down inside that is, and in the preserve of his intimates. His real goal on leaving Russia was America; but lack of funds and trachoma kept him in London. Once he had obtained a footing in his new environment by becoming a regular assistant on a Yiddish anarchist weekly, and in the course of a further year had learned sufficient English to write articles, in addition, in a small commune-anarchist organ, and had simultaneously become the paid secretary of a workers' union, he brought over from his native town of Minsk, his betrothed, Hayyah-Rachel, a small, volatile, clever, interesting woman—and they live together. They have no children, because both regard that as superfluous, something not really necessary. They are, as mentioned, clever people. Taler's chest is narrow and his limbs are small, but his health is always good, and he has never suffered from nerves. His eyes are big and round, calm and protruding, and his smile is cold, twisted, hidden. It appears only when he hears talk about people with ideals, altruism, morality ... Nevertheless, he, Taler himself, talks deliberately and at length on such matters, and in particular, passes judgment on the new trends in social life, on the new relationships between people and between the sexes. He is entitled to. That's his livelihood. Another thing: the workers' unions which he serves as paid president and leader are labelled by him "international"; and Taler, among his friends, permits himself to touch on that with a hint of scorn. He does not find it necessary to pretend that he believes in the principle of internationalism. On the contrary, there are times when he chooses to round off his remarks on this subject in the following manner, stressing individual words at random, whether they are important or not, in his own fashion:

We are talking, gentlemen, about the application of names, and what lurks *beneath* these names. Isn't that so? If then we may be permitted to devote some *attention* to the matter, we may arrive at a conclusion which will in a certain sense be *interesting*, without paying regard to the demagogic impact on us which it engenders to some extent. I do not wish to infer anything from this, and what it touches upon in general, he-he, but nevertheless, I have in mind, he-he, one *little* fact. Now I work, *let us say*, in two workers' unions: the Tailors' Union and the Typesetters' Association. Both of them, as you well know, are *international*, he-he. What *proceeds* from that? One small consequence, a fact: In the Tailors' Union all of us, young and old alike, are Israelites; Beryls and Shmerels, gentlemen—and we have *no* right to our name. *Furthermore*, what is the situation with the Typesetters? Once again, all of them are Jews unquestionably, if we don't count Shtaktorov, and he, too, is bound to *convert* soon. So much, gentlemen, for your fear about the *name*! He-he. In the *International* Tailors' Union there is not even a Shtaktorov ...

And Shtaktorov, Fyodor Shtaktorov of Moscow, one of the few Russian exiles to have dealings with the Jewish ghetto, a sturdy figure with a fair measure of vitality, is clad, both during working hours and in his leisure time in a blue linen tunic, fastened diagonally at the throat by a row of little white bone buttons and tied with a thick red woolen cord whose twisted ends fall in plaits about his loins—Fyodor Shtaktorov's loins. The movement of Shtaktorov's belly as he walks gives the impression of flatulence, and his rear end, begging your pardon, seems too near the ground. Shtaktorov is a mechanic and works in the same printing press as Shalom Lieberman, namely, Crab and Co. Apart from that, he has long held progressive ideas and is not antisemitic at all, having lived for some considerable time among the Jewish students in Bern and Geneva. A loyal socialist, he regards it as a right and duty to be a member of the Association of Typesetters and attends their weekly Friday evening meetings (on Saturday nights the tailors have their meetings!) at Taler's place.

Taler's apartment consists of three rooms: one of them, the master's study complete with desk and newspapers, also contains two beds and a certain amount of furniture; the second, a wide, open hall, designated for meetings, has an iron bedstead in the corner with a straw palliasse, sheet and pillow, and serves as lodgings for my friend Lieberman and myself; the third, which comprises kitchen, dining room and living room, is where Taler's sister sleeps. Eve is a girl of about seventeen, a hat-maker by trade, brown, straight, warm, quick (Lieberman would add, sympathetic) with a mobile face.

That's how it is. Now that I have mentioned Eve, may I be permitted to add an aside concerning her. In the previous section, I recall, I spoke about the "boredom"; and Eve is remarkable in that respect! At present she, too, is unemployed and, having few friends, she stays at home all day. Nevertheless she doesn't appear to find it at all tedious! Whether asleep or just sitting down—she seems to be all expectant, waiting, simmering ... nor does she pay the slightest attention to the clearly expressed dissatisfaction emanating from her brother and sister-in-law at her sitting idle in their home and sponging off them. It doesn't seem to affect her in the slightest, so occupied is she with herself, so full of life and happiness ... thus far.

Let me return to our theme: Taler's apartment. With the help of an English maid, the household is managed with great skill, if not with striking economy, by noisy little Hayyah-Rachel, the former Bundist, and even now an attractive woman, especially when, from time to time, she presents a popular talk at the workers' club. Admittedly, traces of her former life in the party may occasionally be recognized in the Hayyah-Rachel of today even in household matters; but essentially, she is already far-removed from all that! She has finally succumbed completely—I won't say to the family—but to the household! Only her laugh—a high-pitched, unnatural laugh, emitted through thin dry lips—reminds the walls of her apartment of her days gone by ... And within these walls I live too.

And there are times when I reflect:

What this household, just like any other household, needs to soften the damnable unpleasant coarseness is a healthy baby in a cradle—to soothe its crying, look after it, await its smile and its lovely dimpled laugh and surrender to its mystery. But Hayyah-Rachel, the "emancipated" Mrs. Taler is not a mother. Five times a day she calmly consumes the delicacies and dainties prepared by the maid—and Shemaiah Taler is her mate.

"There's vision for you!"

iv

A strange world without God, a strange world and not, in fact, a big one; and in this strange, little world there is another special tiny world—the printing-press of Mr. Isaac Crab. And every day I take myself to the administrative section of "The Daily Crab," at the end of the ground floor of the building where the press is housed, to pick up copies of the paper—Crab's paper.

Crab's paper. In England and the United States the "dailies," "weeklies," "magazines" and "reviews" are called for the most part by their owner's name. And along with its betters: "The Daily Crab."

Crab, the wealthy owner of the daily, is also a Russian Jew, and there are times when instead of "vages" he says "zhalovanie." But he has been a resident of London for more than twenty years. Although well over fifty, he is always clean-shaven, and he even trims his moustache in the English fashion. The wisps of hair around his bald pate can go for months without attention, until they are scythed off one morning without trace. The great man's cronies explain his different attitude towards beard and hair by the fact that whereas shaving is the work of his own hands, a haircut costs money. So when he makes up his mind that the time has come for him to go to the barber for a haircut, he wants his hair reduced to the roots for the price. Stinginess, an old man's stinginess. But otherwise Crab is still virile, and old age has not encroached upon him. His voice is young and pampered, like that of a scion of good family, to the manor born; and in a large and beautiful detached house in a southern district of the city where the English upper classes reside, there lives the daughter of an impoverished aristocrat, to whom, it is said, Crab is paying court. At least Crab tries to foster the impression that this is what they say about him in the city. He talks to her on the office telephone in quite different fashion, dropping hints discreetly but suggestively, in a gentle, unjewish, coquettish voice; and when somebody in this special little world—in any way connected with the paper, happens to wander by chance into those southern city reaches, and passes by that stately home, he says to himself, "That's where our Crab's lady lives"—and feels a surge of pride.

Crab has a reputation in his circle of not being quite right in the head, of not being a typical tycoon, of not being like other people of his age. First and foremost his stinginess has become a byword. But that's not the main thing. The main thing is his violent swings of mood from one moment to the next. Even his assistant, Jacobson, the foreman over the typesetters in the press, a fellow of Galician origin approaching forty, a natty gent with a trim moustache, a fervent advocate of a Jewish hospital, extremely cunning and always clad in Sunday best—even that sycophant declared that no one could rely on the word of his "employer." One thing now, next minute something else. "In a word—unbalanced..."

Even the big clock, on the ground floor shared its master's strange characteristics: every morning at eight o'clock when the men had to appear for work, it managed to be ten minutes fast; in the evening, on the other hand, when it was time to go home, it had for some reason become a quarter of an hour slow ... perhaps there was some unclean hand at work—the gentile caretaker's hand perhaps, Meester Herry, a sturdy little Englishman, who had previously served in the army in India, and now lived in the tidy caretaker's flat with his tall housewifely spouse and their little ailing daughter—but no, no! An Englishman of his type could not be suspected of anything like that. "The clock's mad"—Jacobson affirmed—"mad as its master..."

And the "mad" master would sometimes get up early and come rushing into his press before eight. The great building with its rooms, cubicles, machines, pages and columns, its iron, its boxes of letters all ready, filled, well-ordered, inanimate would appear at such a moment of quiet, glorious and gigantic. And all this stood idle throughout the night, more than twelve hours continuously, bringing in nothing! ... Without so much as a "good morning" to Meester Herry, Mr. Crab raced up floor after floor until he reached the typesetters' section. Why is nobody in yet? Why? It's empty, completely empty ... Isn't Shtaktorov in yet? Not even Jacobson? He knows how frustrating it is ... and Mr. Editor?

Mr. Crab utters the title "Mr. Editor" only for the benefit of the gentile caretaker. In his own mind, and in front of others, he regards that weak, bowed, podgy creature, who gets two pounds a week, Mr. Katlansky—not as editor, but at most his, Crab's, chief assistant; in spite of the fact that Katlansky, for all his grotesque movements, with a handkerchief always tied round his face because of toothache or incipient boils, with his slovenly gait and everything else, was at one time the regular London correspondent of both *Ha-Melitz* and *Ha-Tzefirah* together, whereas he, Mr. Crab reads the news in his own "daily" only with difficulty. That counts for nothing! He is both owner and boss, "Crab and Co." He is the chief, the director, the editor, the policy. And Mr. Katlansky? He is merely the servant who carries out his orders. Just let him try to cross him, Crab, in anything—and the two pounds a week will fly away! Where is Katlansky? It's light already!

But here comes Katlansky and Shtaktorov and Lieberman, here come the apprentices and the rest of the staff; here comes the girl who works in the office, and here, too, comes Eve Taler (she has recently started work here folding the pages) with her heavy tresses wrapped round her head like a garland. Here comes Spinner who "puts the news together," here comes the proof-reader and the rest of the editorial staff; and finally here comes Applebaum the "Meneger," who takes the advertisements and parcels out the papers to the distributors—and Crab calms down at once.

Jacobson! I want the paper out an hour earlier today, by ten at the latest.

How can I? . . . It depends on the editor.

No arguments! . . . Crab took umbrage—there is no editor . . . I'm the editor . . . I won't have the paper coming out at twelve . . . Go and see how many copies get returned unsold . . . Why? . . . I don't want my workers coming so late . . . I'm the boss . . . we'll see . . .

Crab pours out words and phrases without any apparent connection, but with an inner connection—reflecting his thoughts. What follows? Obstinacy, excuses, shouting, firm orders. Katlansky, come here! It's not his fault. Jacobson's to blame. O no!—Jacobson shouts—let's have the copy in time. And Crab threatens: He will stop bringing the paper out. If it's not out in time—he will close the press. He doesn't produce the paper for profit. He never sees any profit from it. He brings it out for the benefit of the public. He, he . . .

And the details, the thousands and thousands of details which go to make up life, go round and round and round . . .

"There's vision for you!"

There's a Crab in the world, there's a paper in the world, whether it comes out earlier, or comes out later—it gives me my daily bread, I live off it, I live off it.

v

I live off it. At eleven o'clock each morning, in company with a gang of newspaper lads of my own age, I return the unsold copies to Applebaum the "Meneger," together with the proceeds—and wait until the "new number" appears. Once it appears, they dole me out the required number of copies; I snatch them up and hurry off to take my place at the corner of Whitechapel and Brick Lane (A street-vendor! It was from that corner that I saw *him* for the second time) and there I stand and call out: Tomorrow's paper! Tomorrow's paper!

Tomorrow's paper. The Sunday edition is headed "Monday," the Monday edition "Tuesday" and so on until the Friday edition which is headed "Sunday." The paper has four pages. The front and back contain big advertisements, those yellow, tasteful advertisements. Inside: news from the English press, both this year's and last year's, put together by Spinner, the newsman, a Jew who spends the rest of his working day teaching the holy tongue according to the English method. Although a jolly man by temperament, he dreams of writing a searing tragedy drawn from the life of emigrants, revolutionaries and members of the self-defense units, and presenting it in the local Yiddish theatre—"which will reduce the audience to a state of hysteria." Katlansky himself, the editor, the "advisor" (at his master's behest he would spend an hour every evening in the office proffering advice to abandoned wives, widows unable to remarry, impoverished Jewish emigrants, suppliants of whatever kind) writes almost every day, at Crab's direct instigation, a column entitled "Seen and Heard" devoted to parliamentary sessions, to matters of state in general, to public institutions in need of support, to local scandals, to the question of ritual baths for Jewish women and to cantors who have gone off the rails. The rest is filled with snippets taken from the "Freynd" and other overseas papers, with romances and penny dreadfuls which are put in the paper lock, stock and barrel without acknowledgment. For the distributors and vendors there is an additional "poster"—an eye-catching announcement summarizing the main feature: "Eighty year old Jew weds fifteen year old girl; English woman strangles her three children and then kills herself; terrible new pogrom in a Jewish community ... a hundred killed and three hundred wounded ... Tomorrow's edition will contain a detailed picture of the slain"—

And I stand on a street-corner in Whitechapel, crying over and over again:

—Buy the paper, Jews ... buy ... the daily ... the daily ... one ha'penny, one ha'penny ... tomorrow's Crab, tomorrow's Crab ...

On my left—the copies; under my arm—the poster with the pogroms, both real and imagined ...

I make my living out of pogroms.

In the evening I go to my lodgings. Good lodgings, a complete contrast to all the rest. The other paper boys do not live in such lodgings. Lieberman is reading by lamplight the copy of the paper which he set, and which he receives free from the office. "Two girls were raped and survived. One girl, called, Marcia Schneider, was raped while dying."

A strange light appears in the reader's eyes.

—Eve is asleep already ...

A moment later he continues:

Shtaktorov was here. He has become too frequent a visitor in this house. Taler spends whole evenings with him. What's Taler up to? I don't understand!

In the workers' union Lieberman always regards it as his duty to stand up for Taler, and to support him to the utmost against his opponents. In private, however, he doesn't think of him as a man who would cultivate anyone's friendship without ulterior motives.

No reason to hate him—Lieberman confesses—but I can't help it. I cannot bear Shtaktorov! I fear that even his sociology is not well grounded. Marxism! He knows a lot about Marxism, that Russian!

—When will you finally give me something to read, Mr. Lieberman—Eve interrupts him, coming out in a well-filled blouse, cosy-looking, full of joy and life.

Aren't you asleep yet, Eve? ... Lieberman tries to appear in control of himself and bravely keeps his gaze level—and I imagined ... Oh! Something to read ...

She returns to her room with light attractive movements, her glance displaying a certain puzzlement and dissatisfaction.

Lieberman lowers his eyes to the paper and says:

Shtaktorov's boorishness makes a very bad impression on me. I cannot bear him. Our landlady, Taler's wife ... doesn't please me either ... where he's concerned. People say: family life, happiness, lifelong companionship—eh!—You should have seen what happened here when that Russian came and Taler wasn't at home ... Hayyah-Rachel ... our mothers weren't like that ... what eyes she made ... she says, she met him in Russia already ... both she, and her husband ... in Russia ...

Old banalities. Faces from the grave. Desolation and conflict, and everything, after all, different in reality from the way it appears. Incomprehensible. A dark pit, terrible fear. Breathing today, breathing tomorrow—all breathing. Feeling the pin-pricks today, feeling tomorrow ... no, tomorrow will be worse, still worse! No strength and nobody. How can I bear it alone, how? To what can I lift up mine eyes, to what? Don't shout ...

"Ha! Vision. Ha, ha, ha ..."

vi

The end of January.

Nothing new. Winter. Coal is dear. Bread, too. A great dispute has broken out in the butchers' shops: rivalry between abattoirs; kosher meat, non-kosher meat. The Zionists levy a subscription for the party. The Suffragettes demand the right to vote. Twelve thousand unemployed wander about the streets. Three are arrested. Elections to some public institution are taking place. Carriages go prancing along the streets. The voters are conveyed in them. Meetings at every street corner. The missionaries, too, make propaganda. Four hundred and fifty six men killed in the iron mines. The world goes on as usual.

Everything proceeds smoothly. Mrs. Hayyah-Rachel has hung new curtains on the windows. This week she went with Shtaktorov to see a new play "The Nazarene." Taler is jealous of her; he is busy every evening with his livelihood. It is as though the word *livelihood* is engraved on his forehead in red ink—in English. Jealousy of his wife is certainly all that remains of his former relationship with her—if there ever was such a relationship. Shtaktorov comes every three days. He has no time—he apologizes—he is busy with his own studies. Taler, for his part, finds it right to cultivate him steadily. Out of fear, perhaps? The working conditions in Crab's place have deteriorated: instead of starting at eight, they now begin at seven o'clock. Rumour has it that he plans to introduce a typesetting machine into his press, which can do the work of six typesetters; and those six, Shalom Lieberman among them, will be left without work. A bright future. For the time being a new typesetter is being sought for some reason. Lieberman says that the notice displayed in the window: "Competent typesetter wanted," has been deliberately planted by Crab to divert attention from the new system he intends to introduce into his press. Lieberman never stops complaining in general. Every Saturday, and every spare moment not occupied with reading the "Daily," he is busy arranging his possessions and complaining. Lieberman has lots of cases, and many shirts, collars, neckties, old newspapers and rags, and he arranges and rearranges his possessions and old clothes from one case to the other, and one place to the other, hanging his many pairs of trousers, vests, shirts sometimes on one peg sometimes on another, hammering new nails into the walls for hanging, sorting out whatever he no longer needs and putting it away in a special place, and next time choosing something else ... Again he has engraved seals of all kinds, large and small, in Yiddish and in Russian, bearing his name and the name of his birthplace: S. Lieberman, Shalom Lieberman, Shalom ben Hayyim Lieberman of Dubno, S.H. Lieberman from the city of Dubno ... and they lie in a special little box, and he frequently busies himself with them. With them—and with his complaints. The cause of his complaining is the same old theme: desolation, emptiness, lack of content. Man, man and his desolation. Lieberman has a sad, special kind of grimace, a pouting of the lips in a particular way, and with this grimace he complains. There's nothing to read. It's impossible to get Russians books, and in Yiddish there's nothing to read. "The Jewish proletariat has nothing to read."—He quotes the sharp comment from the weekly of the Socialist Zionists. Another thing: he used to belong to the association "Eretz" (Land)—he is something of a Territorialist—but there is no life in the association now. "The land has gone to ground"—he jokes. Apart from that he yearns for marriage, and there is no hope of that for him. "For the proletariat"—he remembers another quotation from a different pamphlet—"married life is only a luxury." He knows all kinds of facts. Hell's torments. Hard, enforced abstinence; abstinence from a beloved woman. And indeed, has he the right to beget children? How will he support them? Could he give them a proper education? And anyway, he isn't a healthy man, he suffers somewhat from nerves—has he the right to father generations of nervy, sickly offspring? And anyway—where is it possible to find the right one? He has known very few women in his life ... The clock ticks away, and I, the writer, listen to Lieberman's complaints, delivered in a soft, feeble, downtrodden voice, noting all his considerations: what can he offer a woman, and what can a woman offer him?—And he sinks very low in my esteem.

Moreover, all the easy-going, quiet, moral, feeble people, all the moral "historical," weak, quiet, Jewish-Christian ideas—seem to me some kind of "joke." Can weakness and impotence save us? Long live Eve, long live her characteristic walk, and long live the body she carries! In a somewhat strange, but strong and simple manner she walks and carries her body, her flesh. She returns from work and puts on her dress, a young girl's dress. Lieberman lives in the same house, gives her the "Kreuzer Sonata" to read in an American-Yiddish translation, and refuses to court her—she is amazed at him, amazed. She is mature, and she wants to live. She recognizes from his manner towards her and his movements that he is not at all accustomed to women—and her respect for him declines sharply. No doubt his future wife will benefit from it. Men like him get trodden on by their wives like a doormat, but however it is, he isn't a real person, he isn't a person ...

vii

In short—everything is for the best! No, everything really is for the best! I was ill for two days, and for two days I lay on my sick bed—then I recovered. Lieberman looked after me during my illness, and for all that, it is good to be healthy, good for oneself and good for others—.

viii

Eventually I saw him for the third time! And now that I have found him, really found him, I shall hold on to him, hold on ...

Who knows three?—I know three! Three times, three times ...

That's why I said: It is good to be healthy, good. Give thanks, for it is good!

For had I not been well, I would not have gone to the press to get papers, and had I not gone, I would not have got what I did.

He is very tall, dressed in tatters and his name is Menuhin, Abraham Menuhin. He met me in the street in the morning, when he was wandering about trying to find the way to the alley where Crab's press is housed. He had seen the advertisement in the "Daily" that another typesetter was required. He had the feeling he has already met me ...

—In the "kitchen"?

—Yes. In the "kitchen."

—But only once—I stammered—only once ... he hadn't appeared again ... he wasn't there any more ...

He had been there several times. He had. There was no need for any greater frequency. There was no need for a "kitchen" (with a little smile). They don't let you eat there on credit.

—If I were the owner of the "kitchen"!—a merry, charitable mood enveloped me.

I?—he looked straight at me—that is clear. My face, one might say, he was compelled to say, was of the kind which, when he came across it, he engraved on his heart: One of us ...

He said it with affection.

I laughed aloud with happiness, and a feeling of joy engulfed me. "One of us" ... To tell the truth, I have a similar instinct. But with respect to him ... to term him "one of us" is still not enough, not enough. Such awe and reverence for tall people!

And we walked along together.

★ ★ ★

—And you won't organize strikes against me?—Crab said to him during the interview, and to his surprise received no answer to the loaded question.

To mitigate the unexpected impression, the employer's hand rose to pat his new employee on the shoulder, but for some reason he refrained even from doing that.

—But you are a good typesetter ... a proper typesetter— that's right, isn't it? ... You promise me ... Don't think ... Look, I'm the boss here ... But I'm an intelligent man ... You set type without mistakes? ...

Menuhin answered: mistakes are unavoidable. But mistakes can be rectified as much as possible. He is also a good proof-reader ... if there is a need for it.

—Is that so?—Crab nodded his head—I'm very pleased ...

And he turned to the girl in charge of the books:

Berta! Put this man on our list of employees!

"What is your name?" The English-Jewish girl turned to him in English with that undisguised look of dislike with which an English-Jewish girl considers it her right to greet every Russian Jew; but after looking at the man standing before her for a moment she translated it into halting Yiddish.

He told her. What a voice he has! ... Not mellifluous, not refined, not humble, not pleasant ... but ...

But then the deep inner lament over the death of a beloved mother is not refined nor pleasant, nor is it even nice.—

Never have I heard a man pronounce his name in such an inner, heart-felt, resonant voice. Abraham Menuhin! ...

ix

Sabbath eve. The daughters of Israel have washed and combed their lovely tresses. Our sole consolation. In all the synagogues and prayer rooms in this street—in "The fraternal association of Zribivitsh," in the "Come and let us rejoice, sons of Panorovke," in the "Prayer room of the tent of Jacob" etc., etc., etc., etc., they have welcomed the old Sabbath queen. Even the majority of secular households display external changes. Let them rejoice who find in this some comfort. In our hall, too, Hayyah-Rachel's maid has made all the necessary arrangements under the direction of her mistress. She has spread a dark red embroidered cloth over the little table, with a chair nearby, and placed on it a jug of water and a glass, in the customary manner of public lectures. Only the simple wooden benches remain standing in disarray. The rest of the furniture, apart from our bed in the corner, comprises only a medium-size mirror opposite the door on the right. Eve emerges in all her six dresses, one after the other, ready for a walk. She stands in front of the mirror for a quarter of an hour or more, making minute improvements to her apparel, returning to the inner room and coming out again, until everything is satisfactory—and off she goes. Shalom Lieberman lies fully clothed on the iron bed, day-dreaming. Silence and expectancy. The door opens and Mr. Jacobson comes in from outside, all smartly pressed, and with a rapid gait, as though deliberately to draw attention away from his bowed form. A smile is ready on his lips. At that moment I notice, sideways on, what lips he has, what lips!

Jacobson (with his ready smile): Good evening! A good Sabbath evening to you! A good week to you!

Lieberman (brightly): Mr. Jacobson? Among the first ten!

Jacobson: If not me—who else? Have you many trade-unionists like me?

Lieberman: Mr. Jacobson practices what he preaches. Very good.

Jacobson (rubbing his hands): Is there really no one here yet? (with satisfaction) It's a scandal, a scandal ... The invitation card said "at seven o'clock." You wrote it!

Lieberman: It is strange, isn't it? Soon we shall have to write *six o'clock* on the cards—then it might perhaps be possible to start at eight. It's no good the way I wrote them; if it reads "at seven o'clock," every single member interprets it this way: Since it says "seven o'clock" it means they are aiming at eight o'clock, but they certainly won't begin until after nine, so there's no point in coming before ten ...

Jacobson: Jewish habits ... It's not like that in *their* union. That's why I argue over and over again: we must become affiliated to them ...

Lieberman: That's another item we have to discuss this evening. And so many other important items: the new typesetter at the press, the strike proposal ...

Jacobson: (on his own track) The argument runs: Their general union won't accept us. Why shouldn't it? I admit, their conditions of work are different; none of their workers gets less than thirty nine shillings a week, that's the fixed union rate ... But what of that? On the contrary, that's what makes it likely. Because their conditions are so very much better than ours—they won't want us to undermine the status of the job, and they will accept us, to bring us into line. They will accept us—why shouldn't they accept us?

Lieberman (in a lecturing tone): Every single one of us, if he is qualified, can become a member of their union; but our Jewish union—or "international" if you like—has to be separate. The two unions must be separate. That's my opinion. That's also what Taler always says.

Jacobson: It's a scandal, a scandal. It's eight o'clock—and nobody's here. (with a gesture towards the inner room.) Is he here himself?

Lieberman: Taler? No, he's gone out too. He will come in his own good time.

Jacobson: And Shtaktorov?

Lieberman (angrily): How should I know?

Jacobson: But I know. He won't come ... (suggestively) He hasn't got time ... (with enjoyment) A thief doesn't return to the scene of the crime ... Our young lady goes to him ... every day after work.

Lieberman (sadly): Ah . . . Why talk nonsense?

Jacobson: That's as may be—nonsense or not, I don't mind. But I'm terribly worried. Shtaktorov can do what he likes, so long as the second thing isn't true . . . that affects us all, every one of us . . .

Lieberman: What are you driving at, Mr. Jacobson?

Jacobson: What am I talking about? The typesetting machine Crab is bringing into our press. It's all prepared. We will all be left without bread.

Lieberman: We must discuss that item this evening. But what connection . . . what connection has Shtaktorov got to that?

Jacobson: Naïve people know nothing! They say that Shtaktorov meanwhile and someone else are secretly going to a school for machine typesetting to learn about it properly.

Lieberman: So I've heard, but I don't believe it.

Jacobson (with a smile of amusement): Why not?

Lieberman: Nonsense! Is Shtaktorov going to set in Yiddish?

Jacobson: He will learn. Don't they say about him—a one-time student?

Lieberman: I admit he was a student at a technical school, but he will never learn Yiddish. That sly one has got fists, good fists for fighting, but not for learning languages.

Jacobson (pointedly): That Eve of yours will teach him.

Lieberman: More slander . . . (concealing his distress) And the second one who is supposed to be learning?

Jacobson: Oh, if I only knew! If the old woman were an old man, she wouldn't be an old woman . . . but I guess that the second is the new typesetter.

Lieberman: The new typesetter? (ecstatically) Mr. Jacobson, you don't know the man . . .

Jacobson: And I don't want to know him. In no circumstances should he be working with us. Did you invite him to our meeting?

Lieberman: What a question! He will come. With a man like that, if our organization tells him he is not eligible to work in the press—he won't work. We can be sure about that. For the time being I told him, that until he becomes a member of our union he has no right to work, and he said that he would come and join.

Jacobson (laughing): But who will accept him? I will be the first to vote for his non-acceptance. In the English union the practice is never to accept a member until evidence is produced that he has been engaged in the trade for seven years and that he earns thirty nine shillings a week. And who will vouch for him here? A fine thing! Don't we have enough members of our union out of work? Why should we accept a stranger from outside and give him a nice, snug place?! . . .

Lieberman: And I say, that it is essential to accept a man of his kind on all counts . . . (holding his head) Isn't it marvelous? Our workers deserve a good kick. Well, if they don't come to this evening's meeting from the other presses—I can understand it (sarcastically)—why should it affect them? After all, it's only Crab's workers who will be left without bread—they and no one else, but ours . . .

Jacobson: It's a scandal, a scandal: it's terrible what goes on in our press. Our "madman" is a dictator, and does whatever he fancies. He thinks up extras whenever he likes, without considering whether it's possible for the workers or not. It's all right for the editorial! Katlansky only needs to cut out a few more bits from the American papers—and there it is! But what about us? . . . And who can tell Crab what to do? New typesetters come and take our places, while there isn't even enough work for ourselves—and nobody worries about it. And what's the reason for it? It's all because we have built our own platform, and not become a branch of the general union. Oh, if we were only affiliated to the general union—then it would be a different matter. For the last six months I have been fighting for affiliation to the general union, and my throat is hoarse from talking about it. (taking out his watch) It's nearly half past eight—and nobody's here. I'll go out for a bit too. I'll have a glass of beer at Smith's.

Lieberman: What's wrong with having a drink at Maisey's?

Jacobson: I don't go to Maisey's. I can't bear that crowd of paupers. But don't worry, my dear secretary! It's all right—Jacobson will return in good time. (buttoning up his overcoat)

Lieberman (anxiously): They're all going. (changing from sorrow to elation) But here comes Mr. Taler!

Jacobson (remaining): What can we expect—if the head himself is late ...

Taler (with the usual haste of the busy man): No one here today either? A bad business, gentlemen.

Lieberman: Marvelous, isn't it? Each one opens the door, sees there's nobody here—and goes off. This way we'll never reach any conclusion. And when? Just at the time we have to decide on so many things.

Jacobson: In the English union they levy a fine on anyone who doesn't come to three consecutive meetings, and if he can't produce a good excuse and a satisfactory reason—they expel him from the union.

Taler (with his incorrect emphasis): Comrade Jacobson is *always* on his one track and he forgets that we and the English union are not at all *twin* models. The English union always was, still is, and always will be *Conservative* on principle, while we must strive to ensure that our union takes its stand more and more firmly on the *summit* of progress.

Jacobson (sighing deeply in Taler's face): What can we expect, when our leader is an anarchist, and not a trade-unionist.

Lieberman (in a dismissive, mocking tone): That's the trouble ...

Taler: Mr. Jacobson's remarks—constitute a worthy note

from a worthy member but, I am very happy to say, they are not true. The difference between myself and comrade Jacobson is a difference of principle. Jacobson is a trade-unionist and I, too, am a trade-unionist, but I always endeavor to see that the associations in my charge occupy the very summit in their economic, revolutionary aims, and that they are not merely narrow conservative, professional associations; while Mr. Jacobson regards himself as a loyal and proper trade-unionist only because he earns a wage which others do not earn; a trade-unionist, because he "lives a trade-union life," because he receives a trade-union wage . . .

Jacobson: Thirty nine shillings is still not a real trade-union wage. But I say, it's true: An association of workers has got to be an association of workers; that is to improve the situation, and not to aspire to anarchist aims! And our leader Mr. Taler is, very regrettably—but we must face the truth—an anarchist!

Lieberman: But, God in heaven, how long are we going to argue? We must open the meeting . . .

Jacobson: With what kind of quorum?

Lieberman (with an obstinate smile of triumph): A quorum of three. Isn't it so?

Taler: We shall take the Crab item off the agenda.

Jacobson and Lieberman (simultaneously): How can we?!

Taler: In the first place, there's no time, gentlemen; secondly—we don't yet know anything about the machines Crab is going to bring in and we can't work out any strategy . . . Have either of you spoken to Shtaktorov? We should have consulted him . . . And suppose, for the sake of argument, he brings in one machine—it's not so terrible: From what I've heard, he is going to bring out "The Weekly Crab"—so there will be work. And apart from that, gentlemen—between ourselves—why should we deny it? Do you really imagine it is possible to fight against the introduction of new machines? The days have passed when they used to smash improved means of production; it's impossible to fight industrial progress... in short, we have to wait and see how it will turn out. Next: regarding the worsening of conditions—we can't discuss that either... You see, he-he, regarding the matter of the new typesetter—we have to make an immediate decision about that, without delay. Isn't that so? I admit in principle, he-he, I cannot be against it, if he wants to join our association, and as I said, we can't learn from the English union: we are not a "trust," we are not a "syndicate" ... The main thing, gentlemen, the main issue of the matter under discussion is this, that by bringing a non-union worker into his press, Crab has given us the sign for battle—and for battle we are always ready. We...

Lieberman (interrupting him): You see. I told you he would come... Here is the new typesetter...

Menuhin enters, and sits quietly on one side. The clock strikes nine. Minutes pass. One by one more workers from Crab's press drift in. Shtaktorov is missing. Finally a dozen or so workers from other presses arrive. They stand like sheep, little flocks of sheep. From Smith's pub nearby they bring glasses of beer. Their stiff white collars sparkle on the necks of the sheep-men in their Sabbath best. It's half past nine. The meeting opens. Menuhin sits on ... Nevertheless I take myself outside!

x

Cruelty to animals, cruelty to animals! Just now, when Lieberman is in an ecstasy of love, when all his calculations "Can he be of help to her and can she be of help to him" seem void and insubstantial; when the question "What will happen afterwards? Can a woman like her be faithful to him?" is no longer admissible, "Since he loves her, loves her, loves her in the fullest sense of the word, he cannot look at her calmly ...

not that he desires her ... surprisingly ... he has no animal desire for her ... but" ... etc., etc.; in short, at the time when "He lost his head," and even drew on his meager savings in the Colonial Bank, and began to take great care about his clothes, and began thinking of a walk with her as the one ideal, and began running after her to the theater, and began making an irrevocable decision to pour out his heart to her in a letter, only in a letter—just at that very time, a strike had to be declared in Crab's press, and who can see how such a strike will end! The decision will be ratified at the meeting next Friday night, and perhaps even before then at an "extraordinary meeting." So it's no good ...

And now—Shtaktorov, that same Shtaktorov whom Taler's wife had begun to instruct "for a lark" in so-called German, the Jewish alphabet, English grammar and other things necessary for a "convert," as her husband Shemaiah relates with mock relish. Lieberman could not restrain himself, and told her husband Taler of his double fear about this instruction in that kind of Yiddish ("aping German; Shtaktorov knows a little German from the time he lived in Berne; why should he want to know German anyway?"). There are two inferences to make. In the first place, the rumor is correct that Shtaktorov wants to be the operator of the Jewish typesetting machine; and secondly ... secondly ... who can tell ... Eve ... Eve from a small town in Lithuania is no master of Russian ... neither of them know English ... and so ... to get closer ... Eve ... and Shtaktorov already has a betrothed in town ... perhaps more than one ...

Taler sat proof-reading the new book of rules of the Tailors' Union: "dues, pay, money, dues, pay, money ..." When he heard the names Shtaktorov-Eve, he raised his rheumy eyes and exclaimed:

—My sister? ...

Lieberman's arguments faltered. Perhaps he detected the

note in Shemaiah Taler's voice: my sister—and not my wife, so that's all right then: I am not my sister's keeper ... let her choose whoever she likes ... *We* are not afraid of the "Gentiles" ...

Nor is the good Lieberman happy with Menuhin. The union had not accepted him, Menuhin, and had adopted a firm resolution forbidding him to work in the press—but he refuses to accept the decree and goes on working! He had not expected that from Menuhin. Admittedly he himself, Lieberman, was completely in favor of accepting him, but since his was only an individual opinion, one vote only, and all the rest had voted: No!—it had to be No!—because otherwise—there would be no end to it! They say, too, that Menuhin is the one selected for the nefarious task of learning machine typesetting, and cite as evidence the fact that he leaves work an hour before everyone else. For what reason? But it is hard for Lieberman to believe that. Menuhin is not the kind to pull the wool over people's eyes, and if he were engaged on any such thing—he wouldn't hide it. You can see that the man's not like other people, that the man is unique. But if he wouldn't commit such a wicked act, and it's impossible that he would—it's amazing that he doesn't desist from its fellow: How is it that he doesn't stop working, in view of the firm decree? Agreed nobody wants to starve to death—but in that case, how is Menuhin different from anyone else? Menuhin ought to be Menuhin, and he is not being so ... Lieberman is disturbed ...

xi

It happened many years ago. I was an extramural student, with a volunteer teacher, likewise a former yeshiva student, a pupil in the top grade of the high school, a special person, a man of the spirit ... He was ascetic in his habits, but for a long, long time and with the purest of motives he had aspired to find a young woman to whom his soul might cleave. With such an idea in the recesses of his heart he used to spend the evenings wandering about the streets, the parks and various public places. He would try in expectation to become acquainted with every young lady that he could. The days passed—and the woman did not appear. He reached the age of twenty eight. I was one of his regular visitors. On one occasion at his place I met a gentle young girl of about eighteen, who had come to the capital from her native provincial town to complete her studies. He was captivated by her from the first moment. By the following day the girl had realized it—and she was glad. But before he could say anything to her, on the very night after he had got to know her, he woke up in the middle of the night and felt a pain throughout his spinal column. It wasn't sudden pain—there had been intimations of it for a long time—but his sharp awareness of it was sudden. The happiness of the first flush of love, however, masked the insidious pain for some time, but he could not get rid of it or put an end to it. The pain gnawed at him from the depths, penetrated his being, pierced deeper and deeper. The doctors did not despair—but to no avail. There were days of hope and days of despair, days of terror and distress. To her he did not dare to reveal it all, but I was the one who knew. Finally he just left a little note for the gentle little girl: "Forgive a rotten tree." But his dumb gray face when I found him—I was the first—lying silent on the couch, was like a dreamer. Its expression signified: "Hold back your sighs ... happiness and pain arrived together and together they have passed ..."

I broke out into a cold sweat all over. That same living expression on the face of a dead man who had taken poison, because he had rejected an existence full of shame, I now began to see on the face of a living man, standing and working loyally in Crab's press—on the face of Abraham Menuhin.

I meet him every day.

He is about thirty six years old. He doesn't talk about his past, and I learn some general outlines only incidentally, as, for example, that for some years he was a staunch member of the "Bund" in Lithuania, at the time when "the organization was still inspired with a kind of religious fervor!" That he had later organized self-defense units in the cities of Southern Russia; that he had been exiled to Siberia for three years, and for lack of work, had collected various plants in the deserts and forests. He has never studied botany, and he doesn't know their correct names, but he loves them, and this love enables him to distinguish them and separate them out. Various albums, the work of his own hands, albums of different flowers and various plants are still to be found in his bag.

Incidentally: he knows Taler and his wife from Russia. They even have some memories in common. He also knew Shemaiah Taler's elder brother, an outstanding man, who died of tuberculosis in front of his eyes in Siberia. The dead man had been very attracted to Hayyah-Rachel, Taler's wife, in her youth—she was orphaned of both parents—but she loved another man ... He had, apparently, also met Shtaktorov at that period. But none of them recognize him here now—and he prefers it that way. He likes to observe without being observed. He is not over-fond of an "intelligentsia" milieu.

The intelligentsia, the intelligentsia ... he grinned—in general ... not only ours ... cafe haunters ... professional spouters ... city windbags ... thirsting for polished phrases ... that's what it is, just that.

I mentioned our other acquaintance to him. How quick he was to grasp the nature of every single one of them!

And a few minutes later, our fragmented conversation, consisting mainly of pauses and silences, turned to the wind of change in the new generation of our "intelligentsia" in Russia and other Jewish centers, insofar as we learn about it here from passing rumor: the negation of any restraint; a total cynicism, whose point is not even peace of mind but—pleasure.

Abraham screwed up his eyes, as though enquiring: Might one not just as well look for the snows of yesteryear? Afterwards he said:

—The wind of change ... all wind ... chaff blown by the wind.

And he fell silent. But later in the evening he added some fragmentary remarks on this subject.

Happy the man who does not walk in the preacher's path and who does not strive to direct everyone into the same road, to make each person think alike and have the same yardstick for living. Each individual, whether he has any fixed design or none at all, lives according to his capacity—let each one live according to his capacity! That's the thing. Peace of mind for the individual—pleasure for the individual—what greater justice and truth is there than that—if there is only complete capacity for it? ... That's it ... Peace of mind ... Pleasure ... We find that from earliest times to the present this capacity has been the preserve of inferior people, the insensitive, the cruel, the weak, those dependent on the help of others ... the superior people, the strong, those who are free in body and soul, the paragons—they are the ones who do not have such capacity. I remind him of the new winds blowing, the "new" teaching, which advocated: Life! Life!—But that again is mere *teaching*, words in the mouths of people, whose whole being, for the most part, contradicts them ...

And again I once heard him say something of this kind:

—There is ugliness in the world, there is. And which of the intelligentsia is ugliest? The one whose strength is no strength, and the ground under whose feet is no ground, and who, for all that—by means of clichés—seems, apparently, to have freed himself from his pessimism, from his weakness, so as to be like others, and not go on living like a hanger-on ... The person is despicable, who cannot "live" and pretends that he could, indeed, he really could, as though he could ... The first thing is: to be true to oneself! The person who cannot live, the one who isn't like other people, even if it is from weakness—shouldn't go out of his way to become capable, to become "like others," and if he does so—it becomes comic in the extreme. The pessimist who pretends not to be—is grotestque in the extreme; the pessimist who recognizes what he is—is not grotesque. It is different, if a man really has the strength to transcend pessimism; but who has such strength? It may still be possible to rise above cheap, intellectual skepticism—but who can break the yoke of mystery, emancipate himself from the burden of existence, free himself from the illusions, the caprices, the strivings of life? Certainly, the humdrum, the banal, the life everyone lives does not lead to any bridge. If there are any roads and paths, then at any rate they are different; the paths to the bridge must be quite different. For him, at least, the matter is simple.

xii

The end of February.

The rumor has now been confirmed. At the beginning of May there is going to be a typesetting machine in the press—and livelihoods will vanish. The "meneger" revealed it all in detail. It also became clear from what he said that it was not Menuhin who was learning to be the "operator," but someone else from outside. There were special meetings. Menuhin didn't come, in spite of Mrs. Taler's expressed desire to see him in her home: she had heard much about him, and his name was not unknown to her. They decided to face up to the evil by sending a delegation to Mr. Crab, asking him to commit himself in writing to give his workers three months' notice—should he wish to dismiss them at any time—and to give them full pay for the whole three months; otherwise—they would call a strike at once and cause him damage.—

And so, no more boredom and emptiness in our street! No more dull days, each one exactly like the next! There is a smell of strike and excitement in the air.

xiii

March arrived. The feast of Purim is at hand.

Whenever Hayyah-Rachel is teaching Shtaktorov "Yiddish," and indeed whenever she sits by him, the great difference between Jewish eyes and Gentile eyes is clearly marked: Hayyah-Rachel's eyes are large, wide-open, except that she makes them smaller with her winking, blinking, and all the enchantments she performs with them; Shtaktorov's eyes, on the other hand are two small apertures, two tiny hollows, two narrow slits, except that he sometimes tries to open them, to widen them—and see more comfortably.

And "isn't it marvelous?"—I say, using Lieberman's phrase—Fyodor Shtaktorov is not a man of words, nor perhaps is he very much a man of action, but what he needs he brings to fruition in an elementary, natural way. Not everyone is graced with the gift of the gab. But he, moreover, adheres so fervently to the phrase "have mercy on us," with which he spices every single sentence, that he cannot relate the smallest and most simple matter clearly and properly. Nevertheless—what a talent he has for impressing a girl. Yesterday in Eve's presence he related in his voice which sounds like hammer blows a complete adventure from his past. This adventure interested me because of another aspect, namely, the other characters involved.

Shtaktorov is a native of Moscow, but then, at that time, just before the turn of the century when the monthlies "The New Word" and "Life" were discontinued, and the prevailing

Marxism caught him in its current, the police ordered him to leave his native city, and so he came to the provincial capital M., where he had relatives on his mother's side, well-established merchants, who helped him. He was admitted as a student at the town's technical college, but his progressive views gave him no rest, and he soon became acquainted with the head of the Jewish socialists—the "Bund." The head of the socialists there was a private teacher, Eve's late brother, of blessed memory. She, Eve herself, must still have been a little girl then playing ball, and he, Shtaktorov, does not remember her from those days, and even that Mr. Taler, of blessed memory, he doesn't remember very well. Mr. Taler's brother, the one who is here, differs from that Mr. Taler in many ways. "Have mercy on us!" In short, he, Shtaktorov, was a straightforward soul, afraid of no one, and conspiracy disgusted him. He, needless to say, was the only Marxist in the whole provincial capital M. Well, he soon became known to the local police. His rich relations took him to task, but he didn't listen to them; he reviled them, abused them until, finally, there was no place for him to lodge, and he was forced to hide in the conspirators' room of the local organization. The late Mr. Taler, of blessed memory was, indeed, not happy about it—he was a fanatical Bundist and he hated the Russian Marxists in a dreadful manner—but he had another comrade there, a decent Jew, not "very distinguished," not "one of ours," not an "oi-vey"—and he was on Shtaktorov's side. There were two hectographs in the conspirators' hideout, a box of Yiddish type, a box of Russian type, and a little press—a complete treasury. The second comrade—not Taler—was very smart. His, Shtaktorov's, memory isn't good, and he has completely forgotten the man's name!—he used to sit there all day doing the organizational work of the entire district, and in the evening he would close the room and lock it. To cut a long story short—Shtaktorov slept there a few nights and was arrested. Not pleasant! The questioning and interrogation started. He, Shtaktorov, behaved properly, of course, wonderfully, and didn't name anyone. But how would it end? He was lost ... but, as he finally found out, his friends did not remain idle, and hurried to his relief, to save him. As I have said, Mr. Taler was a real fanatic, and he argued that the lives of comrades should not be endangered for someone in another party—and he, Shtaktorov, was not a "Bundist," but a Russian Marxist—have mercy on us—so what could be done? But in this too, his friend, that same friend defeated him, and it was decided *to rescue him*, to rescue Shtaktorov ... as I said, that man was a real brick ... I wonder where he could be now? He must have fallen along with those killed in the revolution ... many people fell ... in short, "It takes less time in the telling than in the doing." One day they received an order to transfer him, Shtaktorov, from one prison to another, but the transfer was scheduled for the evening, and meanwhile they put him into the guard room—and there he sat. Suddenly a lad who was unknown to him approached the soldier and asked: "Is the prisoner Shtaktorov here?"—"Yes!"—"Please give him this roll and this salt herring." The soldier was a good man and handed him the gift. The conditions in those days, the conditions of arrest, were not so harsh and fraught with suspicion then as they are now: today they wouldn't hand them over, but then they did. "The Jews are good people"— the soldiers agreed among themselves—"they bestow their favors not only on their co-religionists, but on strangers too." Meanwhile he, Shtaktorov, started thinking hard, and got the gray cells working! He turned away where no one could see him, cut the bread in two but found nothing; he pulled the fish apart—aha!, a little message; "Be prepared! Mirabeau." That was the password, meaning ... he understood at once. Eve wouldn't have understood, she says? That's it: but he understood at once. No more was necessary. He, Shtaktorov, in times of danger, was as bold as a tiger. So, good. In the evening two armed soldiers were detailed to escort him to the other prison. It was a dark night and the streets which were almost on the outskirts of the town were deserted. Suddenly ... he is still walking along escorted by the two soldiers, when all of a sudden people are milling round a little way away ... someone passes in front of them and asks: "Who goes there?" It was bad tactics ... the soldiers immediately smelled something fishy and got suspicious; and they moved off the pavement to the middle of the road ... but a moment later, a second figure passes in front of them and cries: "Mirabeau." "What the devil!"—the soldier in charge exclaimed, but he, Shtaktorov, understood that his moment had come. He suddenly gave his guards the slip, and ran. They were not allowed to shoot, because it happened inside the city limits, and they began to shout. Thereupon—as he was told later— four men prepared by the organization who had been standing at the corner of the street, approached them, and brandished sharp knives in front of the soldiers' faces, and the soldiers were helpless and fell silent. Then, Shtaktorov felt a strong hand on his upper arm, and his cap was changed as he was running, to alter his appearance to some extent (he was wearing a technical-college cap, and his rescuer put his own hat on him, a warm sheepskin hat), and ran with him for half an hour through gardens and courtyards until they reached Taler's house. As they entered the room—it was lit only by one small candle—the sweat was rolling off both of them, as it does from cavalry horses during a battle. But they were saved, they were delighted. Have mercy on us. What success, what daring, but his savior and rescuer was a real brick—there's no denying it. A moment later he vanished, because he had a lot more to do that night. (The organization issued a proclamation in honor of the deed, and next morning the whole town was in ferment: the Jews have rescued one of their own, ha-ha-ha-ha!) But before that man of action left, there was an interesting scene, sentimental: my savior and rescuer—he it was who had organized the whole operation!—and Taler fell on each other's necks and kissed each other by turns. Terrible! ... On the next day he, Shtaktorov returned to Moscow by conspiratorial means. And afterwards ...

—Enough now, Fedya!—his listener finally interrupted him—I know you are a hero! Wait and tell me on the way, my hero! Let's go out for a little walk. Are you coming? ...

xiv

The fast of Esther.

Every dog has its day. Now it was the turn of Maisey's "kitchen" or the "Little Commune" as many people call it, because of its lack of space and room (no room for profits, Maisey used to pun), the absence of decor, smartness, waiters in uniform, the external cleanliness and internal filth and all the other features of restaurants in the big world, except that the dirt here is external and internal at one and the same time; and paupers of all kinds sit here with their hats on and enjoy helping themselves from a platter full of hot barley for a halfpenny, and usually on credit. But it is possible to get from the "buffet," served by Maisey himself, meat and dessert and wine and tea and coffee. But even with such items the landlord doesn't assume the air of an hotelier or in his service the manner of a coffee house, but rather he lends a friendly hand, just comradely help. There is no *dame du comptoir* sitting there to look after the accounts, or be in charge of Maisey's cash, and in her place near the door or by the "buffet" he himself sits, lazy, bowed, untidy, disheveled, the man who was once an agricultural laborer in the Argentine and a carpenter in Philadelphia, and who for the last three years has been an innkeeper in London. Since the day his one little daughter died, he has been smitten with gout, and he is merely a broken reed. His sickly, irritable wife works in the scullery like a horse, and he sits in the "kitchen," doling out credit, calling his guests by name, flattering them, scoffing with them, and bitterly cursing all those who ate with him when they were in dire straits, but now their position has improved, have become "aristocrats" and left him, or those who won't pay their debts, and about all of them—he expounds at length, with his eyes rolling in their sockets.

For Maisey, the innkeeper, the strike was like water to a salt-herring. Who would have come here on a fast day? And now the whole house is filled with the glory of honored guests. Is anyone missing? Even Reb Leibush is here. It's no good asking Mr. Leibush to have a bite like the others—he is fasting—but he's here. They are all here. Indeed, they have talked it over and over again—nipped the bloodsucker's head off. Long live the strike at Crab's! Long live the strikers, let them live and eat at Maisey's. Don't worry, Maisey will give credit. Long live the delegation, which wasn't received! Three cheers for the delegation.

The "delegation" is here too, composed of: one, a forty year old Jew with curled sidelocks, a black beard and refined features, who is so delicate that instead of setting type in the normal standing position, his weakness compels him to sit on a high chair; and the second, the old Reb Leibush mentioned above, grey haired and of ruddy complexion, about sixty five, half-deaf, but spritely and with a sturdy, rounded frame, a very unusual phenomenon in typesetting work, a contentious, troublesome man, constantly blinking his eyes as though surprised at being where he is: how did he happen to be here? ... Reb Leibush is a native of Warsaw, Poland, where he worked at a press for forty eight years without a break. He is particularly adept at setting Rashi script, and his fingers and palms are so accustomed to the type-moldings that without protective material and without prior dipping in water he picks them up and puts them wherever he wants them to be. After the disturbances of the recent past he was afraid to remain in the "city of slaughter" and migrated to London with his family. He lives with them and his sustenance is secure, but he doesn't want to give up working "as long as I'm alive, God willing." But he is not at all happy with this press: There's no order! Nothing is as it should be, nothing is in its place, everything's topsy-turvy ... the windows are open ... it's too cold ... and then the electricity ... That he cannot abide at all! ... He would work two extra hours a day, he would prefer to work without spectacles—provided only that this affliction be removed—the electric light ...

This weighty delegation was dispatched to Crab and Co. with the workers' demands concerning the typesetting machine that was being installed ... But it was not received. Crab was angry. He wasn't von Plehve, to have petitions sent to him. Anyone who wanted to raise a matter with him—should come and talk. Each individual could come and talk. He was the boss, and he didn't owe anything to anyone. Do you see? The "Anglo-Jewish Association" sends delegations wherever necessary, and so the "union" of beggars also sends delegations. He doesn't receive them!

So the strike was declared. For three days now the "Daily" hasn't appeared. Crab runs like a madman from his home to the press, and from the press to the courts and back over and over, alarmed and upset. Applebaum the "meneger" goes round looking for blacklegs, and finds some, but not enough to set the whole paper. The striking workers—vacillating—fill Maisey's "kitchen," drink tea, discuss secret strategy, entice the newspaper lads not to distribute the Purim number should it by any chance appear, post pickets at the door of the press to observe the comings and goings, assume the stern expressions of martyrs for a cause and, in actual fact, enjoy the cessation of work, the days of idleness, the strike pay which for the time being they receive from the union fund; about the central issue—they argue, complain, grumble. Everyone is in a state of agitation. The general view, represented by Maisey, prevails. Anyone who feels uneasy refrains from expressing his opinion other than in hints, in muttered tones . . .

First worker: How will it end? . . .
Second worker: Badly . . .
Third worker: Will he meet all our demands? . . .
Fourth worker: Of course he will . . .
Fifth worker: We'll be lucky if he meets half of them . . .
Sixth worker: We have asked for a lot . . .
Maisey: What? . . . You've asked for a lot? Hm . . . *How* have you asked for a lot? Five demands—that's a lot?! . . . What are the demands? . . . The demands are: 1) The delegation's demand that he should give three months' notice. 2) That the new typesetter should be removed at once. 3) Hours of work as formerly—from eight o'clock to seven. 4) Good behavior. 5) Making good the damage caused by the stoppage .—Well, is that a lot? . . .

First worker: If we lose the strike—I know whose fault it will be.
Second worker: One of our pickets was struck by a policeman.
Third worker: Of course, even the police are on his side . . .
Fourth worker: But did you see our proclamation? Taler knows how to write: "Pharaoh, King of Egypt, in London" . . .
Fifth worker: But they say that Crab is going to sue our union: He shouldn't have written that . . .
Sixth worker: They have also issued a proclamation—it's Katlansky's work: they apologize for not receiving the delegation . . . but they are right to some extent: a lady in a motor-car was waiting at the gate for Crab at the time when our men went to him . . .

Maisey: A lady in a motor-car? To hell with the lady and her motor-car. When the workers send a delegation, it's his duty to receive it, and not to look after ladies.

First worker: It must have been the lord's daughter, his ladylove in the motor-car . . .

Second worker: It wasn't a motor-car. It was a carriage and pair.

Third worker: And I say: a motor-car.

Fourth worker: In their proclamation it says "motor-car," but who knows what it was . . .

Jacobson: Now the madman can really run round shouting: I'm the boss here . . .

Fifth worker: It's not clear yet who's winning . . .

Sixth worker: Who knows if they won't find other blacklegs . . .

Maisey: What? Blacklegs? And don't you know what happens to blacklegs? Did you see the funeral in this street a few days ago? That was the funeral of Herris the tailor, who got a great box on the ear during the tailors' general strike.—"Herris! What are you doing? Why are you going to work?"—I asked him at the time.—"I don't want my little children to starve"—he told me. Well, he won't be worrying about them now. Don't you worry about them either: they are starving all right . . . do you understand? They gave him one box on the ear, he was ill for six months—and died. That's what they do to blacklegs. And you . . . what? (resuming) Is the new typesetter working? I don't see him here . . .

Jacobson: He probably would be working, only he's afraid. Shtaktorov said he would kill anyone who dared to blackleg . . .

Lieberman (who is not at all happy about the whole business): Menuhin is not afraid of Shtaktorov. He isn't working because it doesn't matter to him if he doesn't work for a few days. Doesn't he take one hour off each working day in any case? But he says openly without any hesitation that

Crab is right. Admittedly, our employer should not have resorted to guile in concealing the fact that he was bringing in a typesetting machine, but in this strike he is right ...

Jacobson: He'd better not say that in Shtaktorov's hearing: A box on the ear is a catching disease ... isn't that so, Mr. Maisey? Did you see how he honored the member of our delegation who came back trembling and said that he was going back to work, because when we've lost—we've lost ... he was lucky he didn't get all his teeth knocked out ... (with exaggerated pathos) ... Indeed, the strike can only be lost through treachery on our side! In my opinion, we must apply to the general union, the English one, for help; if it will support us—then we shall win.

Taler (approaches from another group): For our union, gentlemen, the Crab affair is a matter of life and death. *To be or not to be*, as the English say. Either him or us. He is starting a law-suit against us—and that's bad. Comrade Jacobson says: let us apply to the English union. But we must not forget, gentlemen, that the English union is only a syndicate, and not a revolutionary workers' union. As for us—we must not compromise: deals, compromise—God forbid! The trouble is that the union's coffers are empty, comrades, and from now on each one of us can only get sixpence a day strike pay, and it is impossible to live on sixpence, especially for people with families. We must, therefore, discuss what to do. We must apply to other unions for help, the international tailors' union ... we must send a new delegation ... Jacobson and I will go ...

First worker: Of course ...

Second worker: What more needs to be said?

Third worker: Sixpence is virtually nothing ...

Fourth worker: It wouldn't harm anyone to end the business ...

Fifth worker: They say the weekly was due to appear next week ... There would have been work! ...

Sixth worker: The only way is to send another delegation...
Old Reb Leibush (sits fasting).

xv

I am mistaken about him—Abraham Menuhin told me with reference to himself—he is not gentle and he is not one of those who worry about the world. Those who worry about the world worry about the whole world, and they want the world to be just as they want it, while as for him—his world is only what he sees in front of his face, and he pays no attention to the rest. He is not a moralist, although he is not afraid of the word "morality," and he does not regard those who kick over the traces as the choicest of men ("people who carry every burden and people who kick over all the traces—end up the same way"). And in good *deeds*, in desirable relationships he, indeed, sees the one thing without which there is nothing ... in any case, why should I define it when, for the most part, definition is false. If he knows anything about himself, there are, perhaps, two features, both negative: He is not a driven leaf, and he doesn't like doing things by halves. By temperament he is strong and obstinate, and he is brazen-faced ... a certain strength of mind, a certain energy ... well, it's getting comic: we have talked about ourselves enough ... even though, on the other hand, there is nothing else to do at the moment ... let's go to his place ... and loll about on the bed a bit ... he is not afraid of solitude, far, far from it, but his lodging is depressing.

Abraham Menuhin's landlady is, indeed, an unpleasant woman. She is probably not yet forty—but she is already a mass of wrinkles and flattery. When there is nobody with him, she comes into his room with her grown-up daughter to pour out her heart to him and tell him things which "she couldn't say to anyone else." Clearly, if there were any other bachelor living there—she wouldn't be able to say them to anyone else but him. Menuhin controls himself, and gives no expression to the feeling of revulsion which sweeps over him in spite of himself; and perhaps no such feeling sweeps over him at all—who knows ... The woman's tragedy is that she has a daughter, and she considers it her duty to put her on show whenever she meets anyone ... The daughter—is an Anglo-Jewish girl, shallow and idle, lustful, coquettish and silly, and I myself particularly cannot abide her fat chin and greasy hair ... Menuhin's landlady is a widow, living off the charity of her relatives, and she gives us no peace concerning her former wealth in those days, and her daughter's level of culture ... her daughter's education constitutes the foremost concern in her life, she says ... she should be taught French and German—alas! ... and an entrance into Abraham's room is also effected by various stratagems. One evening—the daughter will come in first apparently to look for something in their wardrobe which stands in the room, and the mother comes in after her to see how she is faring—and stays ... Next day—the mother comes in first to greet the "gentlemen" with a "good evening," and the daughter calls "Modder! Modder!" from behind the wall—until she comes in too ... "My daughter, bless her, can't be without me!" the poor, wrinkled mouth smiles ... Abraham paid the rent, and mother and daughter hurried off to buy a white "mantel," which is hung in the wardrobe in his room, and the visits to inspect the "mantel," to try it on and take it off, to fasten the big buttons, become more frequent. "My daughter isn't one for going out—the poor old woman apparently complains—she is a wonderful girl ... (namely: and you should regard her visits to your room as an honour ...) she can't leave her mother even for a moment ... *espechelly*, my daughter's spirit is depressed this winter ... last year a student at the Rabbinical College lodged here ... my husband, God rest his soul, was still alive then, but he was a "dealer" in his old age ... you are "greenhorns," and I don't suppose you know what a "dealer" is? Dealer—is a man who buys things second-hand—we used to be big merchants and we lived in Leeds, but our shop was burned down and we lost everything ... Well, my husband wasn't satisfied with the student in our house ... He—my husband, God rest his soul!—was already dying, and coughing all night, and they, the young folk, used to sit up late, studying together, laughing, he was teaching her French, as is proper these days—I've got eyes and I could see that the student couldn't live a single hour without my daughter ... if my daughter didn't sit down to eat, he would in no event sit down—he used to eat at my table ... Every morning, as soon as he woke up, he used to come out in his underwear, forgive me ... how is she, how is my daughter? ... When his college friends used to come and start talking to my daughter, he was overcome with jealousy and he used to growl at them: "You've come to see me, not Betty, not my landlady's daughter" ... You see how far things had gone! ... What can you say—the boys today ... And my daughter loved him too, loved him—why deny it ... Did she look like this then? She's healthy even now, thank God, when she's not herself, but ... not that ... her head aches almost all the time, she has a pain in her chest, and her hair is falling out ... oh, her hair ... two plaits she had ... they used to go twice round her head ... what can you do ... she can't forget ... "But, modder, she complains, modder, why doesn't he even write, why? He's at Oxford now—why doesn't he write? Is that the way an honorable man behaves?" You can see for yourself ..."

—Modder—the girl-victim sighs, standing on the threshold, with outstretched neck and grief in her eyes, grief without a spark, the black grief of a dice-player, who has staked his all on a throw—and lost everything. The fond dreams of a husband earning four pounds a week, of endless "mantels," of two maids, of universal envy, of Drury Lane theaters—vanished, vanished. Everything is lost. Nightmares followed by empty mornings ...

—If a lodging is no good, change it—he, Abraham Menuhin said to me—that he knows, but here it's not possible—his lodging has one additional virtue, namely, at night he can bring in anyone he wants—without any interference ... even that girl standing in the doorway—prevents it ... you can't just leave girls in need of help "standing in the doorway" ...

—Wrong?

Not "wrong," not "you've no right," not "a person ought"—even if the words displease those clever-dicks who have leafed through books on philosophy, or composed books on philosophy, and their souls—are swirling dust. But that's how it is, like that. Man is *not* created upright in their empty sense. And even if "upright"—certainly not uncomplicated. An uncomplicated soul—that's a mistake. The yea is not on the side of the uncomplicated. The matter is apparently so simple: a male needs a female, a female needs a male, to nourish her body with meat and wine—and life puts its stamp on it, its watchword: simplicity. But it's a mistake. When he was a lad of fifteen, sixteen, seventeen, in a big city, and in a certain milieu—it seemed simple enough to him too, normal. Due to his robust constitution, he didn't fall ill, even though he overdid it for five years in succession. But on one occasion he stayed over in a certain "house" for four consecutive nights, and on the fifth day he got up in the morning and asked himself: "What am I doing?"—and after that he never retraced his steps. Shortly afterwards he met that other Taler and became friendly with him, and that Taler introduced him to the supreme happiness—and he began to see things differently. No. Not to expound in public (a person doesn't teach his fellow anything), not to grasp the horns of the universal imperative, not to lose sight, in the end, of the tragedy which is at the bottom of everything, *of the tragedy which is unavoidable*—only to recognize that this is how it is, this is it. This is how it is, this is the essence of it—and it can't be otherwise. He and that Taler were the leaders of the local central committee. Two bodies—and one soul. A little woman came between them. Now—by chance—he sees the woman sometimes, even meets her, knows what has happened to her, and understands the inherent absurdity of it. But then she was all pure and holy grace. So it seemed. Taler was captivated by her, while she, the little one, was attracted to him, Menuhin. It was a difficult test—and harsh words passed between them. Between the "rivals," the "competitors," there were harsh, unpleasant words, hurtful, spiteful, smoking with envy and revenge, harsh words which arose of their own volition over every little question, over every detail no matter how small. If one of them said one thing—it was understood that the other would say the opposite. Very sad! Meanwhile, that little woman, of whose imagined innocence both of them were convinced, prevaricated, looked on and waited. There was no way out, and who knows how it might have ended ... One day a rescue-attempt came under discussion. Taler said "No," the rescue should *not* be attempted, but even that "no" was not said objectively, but only because if he said "yes," Menuhin would have to be one of the rescue-party, and Taler didn't want to endanger the life of his friend and rival; and again because of that woman: if Menuhin were to succeed—he would be madly jealous, and should he fall a victim—what would happen to her affections then? ... No, no, no attempt must be made ... Life is full of horrors. But an elation of spirit can resolve any impasse. He, Menuhin, in the hot blood of youth, jumped straight into the whirlpool, brought it off, and took the rescued man right back to Taler's room! ... They are after us—so you are in danger with me! Our lives are in danger! Friend and brother! ... And Taler understood. He had not expected that—and the whole dreadful breach was healed in a twinkling. Complete harmony was reached, achieved in one moment. Each of us fell on the neck of his brother and rival—and the dark, dread room was filled with light. Their bodies were of necessity separated, by decree of the thing they served, that very night—but their souls were now inseparable for ever, inseparable ... welded forever with one fiery kiss ... that kiss ... who can grasp its nature ...

xvi

A wonderful find. The torn overcoat, in which Menuhin was clothed all winter, was an inheritance from Taler, that same Taler, the late Taler. Because of the spring warmth Abraham had taken it off, and both of us had used it as a blanket on the night I stayed with him. In the morning, after he had gone to work, I unintentionally thrust my foot into a split in the lining—and made it bigger. Fragments of old letters tumbled out like messages from heaven, letters that had never been finished or sent to their destination, all of them signed with a Latin T. According to the date they carry, they had been written in Siberia in the last year of his life, when he no longer belonged to any organization. They make mention, too, of the names of Shemaiah, the writer's brother, his sister Eve and also Hayyah-Rachel. The writing is crabbed, in Russian script and difficult to read, but here and there I find a few passages in a clear Jewish script written on the pages of a diary. One of them, for example, bears the heading, "A kind of foreword to the testament of a spiritual vagrant," and it begins: "And those days, Abraham my son, are not in truth far distant from me"—

And further on:

"But I am not now going to tell you, Abraham, about the change which has taken place in me since that time, for the truth is that people do not change in essence, and the soul is nourished only by what was in it when it was first created"—

After much erasing it continues:

"... All that remains from those days is: Responsibility to everyone and for everyone—and compassion ...

"Compassion ... that's the word ... it won't leave me alone ... and yet in those days it aroused in me only scorn ... condescension! ... I used to shrug my shoulders, and settle my glasses on my aching eyes and my bulging nose ...

"I was firm in my opinions, with harsh words on my tongue. In my heart of hearts, indeed, the God of compassion and grace had never ceased to rule, but outwardly, in all the manifestations of my life there were: aloofness, anger, pride, scorn for all bourgeois life and all bourgeoisie. Cruelty was even then a stranger to me, the descendant of Abraham, Isaac and Jacob, and although this one quality had no place in my make-up, there was a certain hardness in me, a hardness, which made me judge everything in the severest light where I was concerned, a hardness that would brook no compromise, that engraved marks on people's foreheads: This one is bourgeois, that one is base, the other believes in nonsense—and so: they must suffer the consequences of their actions—

"Listen, Abraham! Don't be upset, have no fear, be not afraid, my good son! I do not mean to tell you, God forbid, that I am no longer aloof and that I have become an organ-grinder (is there such a thing in Siberia?), that hardness and mockery, those pure sisters, have abandoned me, and that I have become indifferent to everything, that I have forfeited anger, pride, and all those praiseworthy qualities that elevate existence—

"God forbid! Everything that was in me then, is in me now; moreover everything that is in me now, was in me then. As long as there is breath in me still, as long as I continue of necessity to be, there is room only for new manifestations and not for any *creatio ex nihilo* ... And indeed, I tell this only to inform you of what has been added to me, added and not born, added because my spectacles have broken from my bulging nose and my eyes drip with sorrow ...

"*She* ..."

A few blurred lines—and again:

"A pity, Abraham, that I cannot tell you everything in one breath. To make you understand (insofar as it is possible at all to understand the soul of someone else) all that I want to tell, I would have to tell it all in one breath, I would have to remove all the husks, all the various descriptions, all the concealments, which are not really relevant. But, my friend, we do not have control of our fate, and we cannot express everything we would like, and in the way we would like it. And you, who are close to my heart, are very well aware that we usually have to follow a sideways path, and it is full of pitfalls, and sometimes we sink in the mire; and the Lord of compassion, my dear brother, will make atonement for us, his wretched children"—

The following section is torn.

And further on, on the last page of the journal, it states: "A few words by a man who has gone to his last resting place." The style is even more confused, and a religious ecstasy pulsates in it. Here is the beginning:

"My end is near—I have taken stock. For once Purim has passed—there is much rejoicing and joy of soul. Thus I decree, Abraham! I who am worthy of His revelations, may He be praised, and I who am prepared and ready to receive instruction from Him, I am alive, I exist. Now that Purim has gone, and we are no longer obliged to say "Cursed be Haman and blessed be Mordechai," and we have overcome the mortal foe, our "district commander," and the power of Bigtan and Teresh and his eunuchs and the behind of his enemy who sits at the king's gate, and we have forgotten all their affairs, their preoccupations and their devotion, and we have cast off our winter clothes, in spite of the terrible, biting cold, and we have finished the meetings and the speeches and the appeals in Minsk, and we have our heads in the clouds—Abraham! Abraham!

"Heads in the clouds and rain and wind. Each day follows the next, each day brings different clouds, each day sprouts and grows, each day brings its sacrifice.—Abraham, here I am!

"April. Halleluyah! Every soul praises God! And if there is no refuge from the vulgarity in the tents, if there is no escape from the filth in the yards; if there is no way from the crushed defilement which arises from the markets (there are markets there and hunger here—one depends on the other), if there is no shelter or cover from the daily tumult—there is nevertheless a quiet corner for the Lord of hosts, there is a break of day for the Lord of hosts, there is a me for the Lord of hosts.

"And if you venture to say: There is *no* Lord of hosts—there is a me . . .

"Me, that is to say, Abraham and me and our Siberian corner, and our break of day, and the Lord of hosts in us. And after the conclusion of our night-long wanderings, and after we have finished seeing everything that no eye is given to see, and after the threads of intervals which come and embrace the kingdom of darkness, then—before the first light of daybreak—there are times when we gather in our corner on that stone and wait for revelation . . .

"And I know, I, Abraham! I who am worthy of His revelations, may He be praised, etc., as written above; for one like me is surely important and welcome and accepted, and our being in this world is surely good and there is no higher

degree in the created world than our longing for exaltation and for revelation and for a ray of light—
"By the way: all my bones declare, that *we* are the ray of light in this world, and that we exist, we and our longing for revelation—
"And I cry out: Be revealed!
"Abraham! Abraham!—And he said: Here I am.
"And I know that day will not be far away!—" ...

xvii

Everything's in order, but since the beginning of April—it's already the fourth day of Passover—I am living alone. Lieberman has left, not wishing to dwell under the same roof as Taler, who "had handed the strike to Crab, when the public at large was on our side, and had destroyed the whole union with his own hands." Never mind, Jacobson had remained true to his beliefs: The English union had ruled that Crab was right: it is impossible to halt the march of industry—and had declined to come to their aid, and so he, the "Englishman," had gone and sold himself to the boss, out of respect for the ruling ... but Taler—What had that got to do with Taler?! ... Lieberman is unemployed now, eating "whatever comes to hand," sleeping at Menuhin's, and wandering about all day from the Zionist reading-room to the English reading-room, and from there to the two reading-rooms of the missionaries —then back to the Zionist reading-room. Nevertheless, he hopes to get work soon. Life, in fact, is not so bad as people might imagine ...

Taler's family, too, is soon to move from its present quarters to the north of the city—to Stoke Newington. The tailors' union is growing, and the present hall is too small for it, and it wants to rent another "locale," which would not belong to Taler. Apart from that dissatisfied voices are raised here and there against Taler in general because he "undermined the workers' union in the East End, and changed his colors; now all he needs is to become an official Zionist!" And indeed, not long ago, when the Bundist emissary came from the organization called "The Awakener," a branch of the Bund, a lady emissary like a black wingless bird, to collect money in the International Tailors' Union for the "Fighting Fund," as always in the past, Taler did not allow her to carry out her design, and delivered a speech to the effect that the workers' union had come about solely to improve the economic position, and not for revolutionary purposes. What a pity Mr. Jacobson was not at that meeting!

xviii

The indignation of the guests at Maisey's breaks all bounds. Crab has brought in not merely one typesetting machine, but two; one for the daily and one for the weekly and any occasional work; the operator of one of them will be Shtaktorov, of the second—Jacobson. The editor of the weekly will be—Taler! How dreadful and how strange!

xix

Summer, summer ... The weather was calm in deference to summer, a little less raw, a little less misty, but still ... still—hard, but not the worst ... not so bad that it takes away almost all desire to write things down ... No! One can live, one can ... and particularly in a quiet, clean street, near a park, such as the one in which Taler dwells ...

Idyll upon idyll. On the ground floor there lives a member of the Anglo-Jewish clergy, the father of many lovely daughters, of whom the eldest was recently married to a young gentleman with an Oxford degree, who lives with his father-in-law. The head of the family is a good-hearted, contented man, who is busy composing a commentary on the Five Books of Moses entitled "Gladness and Joy," part of which has already gone to press, to the gladness and joy of old Reb Leibush, whose soul longs so avidly for work in Rashi script, and also to the benefit, indeed salvation, of my Abraham who would not otherwise have known what to do: now he earns a living from proof-reading the book, as well as proof-reading the weekly which has been entrusted to him. In short, it's good all round. The lovely girls, however, have heard from their mother, that their father the "reverend" is investing a lot of money in it—and to them it seems a very painful riddle ... why invest money in such an incomprehensible thing, when there are so many other needs ... But their distress soon passes: after all they have complete faith that father the "reverend" would never do anything that did not bear fruit ...

So much for the ground floor. Upstairs lives Mr. Taler, the editor of Crab's weekly—he and Hayyah-Rachel, his wife. Eve has been left in the East End with one of her friends, for Stoke Newington is a long way from the press, and she is employed there folding newspapers from morning till night. The expenses in the new place are great, the honorarium for editing the weekly is for the time being small—and it is not possible to let the sister—sister-in-law— give up working. In any case, people in London don't stay idle. A girl has to earn her own living. One has to count the pennies. Especially now with the "new order," in a new place ... admittedly some unpleasantnesses do occur, the unfamiliarity of the place, and in the courtyard—the noise of some Talmudic College, but in general—thank heaven we're out of the East End! The folk there are so importunate, they come and fill the house ... how nice to be alone and only receive selected visitors from time to time! ... Hayyah-Rachel no longer has any contact or dealings with the "Lane" in Wentworth Street, apart from sending the maid there to buy victuals. Then she accompanies her to the steps, telling her with great deliberation and anxiety: "Look here now ... You buy the meat there in the first butcher's, and at the corner you'll find parsley ... but it must be thin parsley ... do you understand? Hayyah-Rachel rubs her fingers together, conveying the thinness of the parsley like an old housewife. The question of lunch for the man who will be coming from the editorial office in a few hours has, apparently, become much more important than the dispute with the bolshevik "Iskra" of many years ago.—

★   ★   ★

And in Menuhin's old room—there is a whole colony of "Russians": himself, Lieberman, myself, others ... his unlovely landlady isn't strict about it: she likes a lot of men milling round not far from her daughter ... and even if the men are poor—Russians can do anything ... strange people ... today they are poor, and tomorrow—who knows ...

We all have time on our hands—and our Father Abraham (that's what we call him) likes living and knows how to live. He says:

We were talking, I believe, about enjoyment a little while ago. When it comes to it, the only thing we really have in our world is pleasure. I, for example, take pleasure at this time in my strength, in my health. Sometimes when I go out and the sun is shining, I automatically lift up my hands in the air. I take pleasure in their strength, in the life they have—in the wholeness in me.

All of us go out very frequently. Outings and long walks on the banks of the river Thames. What are the English to us? Bread we buy in plenty, in joy, with much deliberation. Hot water and bread in plenty. Merry turns round the room without shoes, barefoot. We are nourished off "Gladness and Joy." Life proceeds, ha-ha ... to hell with the writing!

xx

When Menuhin goes off to read his proofs, I sometimes leaf over his albums of plants. It's amazing from where this green takes suck and lives ...

He is fond of plant growth for its own sake—he told me yesterday in his clear, low, deep, quiet voice as we sat in the porch after midnight—He might say: very fond of them. Plants, nice grasses, spring, summer—that's all life can give, isn't it? Life is limited in its scope and limited in its possibilities; one shouldn't ask of it other things, other happiness, one shouldn't ask of it more than it can give. That's how it is, that's it. Here the plant kingdom fulfills them. Here is the boundary, too, of animal life; this is as far as you come! That's how it is, that's it. *Man*—he says—man, not a God-man, not a superman, not an animal-man. Be especially careful not to make demands of an animal-man, but beware of the vegetable-man too. Man born of woman is not a vegetable, he can't just be a vegetable (pause). Do I, his audience, know what he is spouting about? Would it not be better to sit silent awhile? (again a pause). It once happened—it was many years ago and he, it seems, has already told me—that he went and freed from the authorities a man born of woman, who was likely to have suffered heavily; and now, yesterday evening, he had met him while he was busy with a certain maid, and he saw that he wasn't a man, but an animal-vegetable. The relationship of *man* to the female of the species is one. He, Menuhin, is healthy, healthy down to the very last fiber and sinew, and he has the right to say this. Clearly there's no point in regretting that he risked his life for that one, but it was a mistake. The thrill at the time was, indeed, the act of rescue in itself, in the devotion that goes into such a rescue, and not in its consequences! ... Yet, nevertheless ... Ach, yes, yes ... there's no life of happiness, no happiness in life, even if death is not mentioned; but there is happiness, and real happiness, at certain moments. There is momentary happiness. Heroism is not a matter of a moment, but of continuity, but happiness ... That's how it is, that's it.

Heroism ... yes, yes, his life in Siberia taught him: heroism is not a matter of a moment but of continuity, of a constant *Yes* in everyday activities and everyday life. He knows from experience: it is easy enough to be brave for a short time, to withstand one severe test, to dedicate oneself to the performance of one forbidden action, to go out in a defense unit against a band of murderers in uniform or not, and even to go to the gallows. But when he began to live on the Siberian steppes one day, two days, three days, four days, and to worry every day about not starving to death, and every single day to see the desolation all about, to be tormented every single hour by the Siberian exile with all its details and its pettinesses, and nevertheless, not to regret the earlier things, not to let the spirit fail—then he understood, that the highest level is: to stand guard over the importance of man without cease, hours, months, years, to relate as a resolute man to every encounter also—and especially—with young children, weaklings, handicapped folk ... to become a father figure to all the world's bereavement, and not merely for a moment, but for days, for years. Would his heart stand firm if he were to come across it in reality—That is the thing, the only thing to worry about, except for the general worry of undesirable qualities. The need for this—he knows well—stems from his own essence; this need, to be like this and not different, is his own, it didn't come to him from the outside, but what of it—would he really be able to? His particular strength lies in this, that he does not depend on minor, external impediments, that he is not afraid of various unpleasantnesses that face him on the way ... But all the same ... Is that enough? ... Ach. Is that so? Two o'clock already ... nearly dawn ...

xxi

July. "The Weeks of Mourning." Distress.

In actual fact, nothing happened, or if it did—what happened had to happen, what was obvious from the beginning. And nevertheless—distress, distress ...

What happened had to happen. She was eighteen, a hot-blooded girl and not the most level-headed. She hung around and hung around the Jewish boys in the press, at meetings, at concerts, and they fobbed her off with trifles: a book to read, a socialist comment, a compliment, at the most—a packet of sweets. Friend Lieberman was on the horizon, but even he gradually became more distant ... He never tried to touch her even with his little finger! God made the "uncircumcised" different.

What happened was obvious from the beginning:

Shtaktorov promised her something initially, and now he has gone back on it, or the whole thing was done, as is usually the case, without specific promises, but with blind appeal, pleasant words and vague promises that everything would be all right—what difference does it make? Shtaktorov's "characteristics" are not the world's most intriguing topic. The main thing is that *now* Shtaktorov has two answers. One: he is not sure that he is the guilty party ... Secondly: he has no intention of getting married ...

Even brother Taler's wisdom has vanished on this occasion. He always used to say as though in all innocence:

—What a pity I'm married; what a pity I'm married. A prisoner in chains. Anyway, what of it that I'm married. Just because I have my own garden—does that mean that I can't go for a stroll in another garden? Only my Hayyah-Rachel could think like that. This world, gentlemen, is a banqueting hall. Pluck a maiden! Pluck a woman! Stretch out your hand and pluck! Nature is wiser than we are. Nature doesn't want to know about social considerations.

Now he is enraged:

—If Shtaktorov is an honest man—well and good, and if not I'll sue him! ... In England things like this don't go unpunished ...

Sue me ... Shtaktorov emits a full-throated Ho-ho-ho. He knows well enough that it won't be easy for Taler to make a public scandal: a man who occupies a public position ...

The matter has not yet become general gossip. But she, the wretched happy recipient, reveals her secret to everyone unintentionally. Her cheeks have fallen in, she has no face, and the outlines of her figure seem to have blurred. Her back weighs heavy, and her eyes have grown wide.

Distress. Distress. Distress.

xxii

Who can look on Lieberman's grief! Who can look on his grief? The man has no place. He has even stopped reading. He has even forgotten to occupy himself with his engraved signatures. Even his work during the recent past of putting pictures on post-cards from a block bearing a likeness of himself—something which has come widely into fashion—has been abandoned. Day and night he frets in his room.

During the last few months he had almost started to forget her—and to calm down. His attachment to Menuhin had helped a lot. Now—the wounds have been reopened.

The moment he first heard the tidings he looked as though he had been struck on the head with a hammer.—"Marvelous! I knew it would come to that!"—the words escaped his lips at once with a kind of satisfaction ... But the very next moment those lips became so pale that the bystanders turned aside so as not to see!—"There's no escape from the 'gentiles', no escape ... even here they pursue us, pursue our daughters" ... He, Lieberman, can't bear it any more ... he must fly from here ... he still has a little money ... He will go to America. He will make his way to Palestine.—

In the press there are whisperings—and laughter. Shtaktorov has gone up in everyone's estimation, even though they certainly don't like him. Their attitude to Eve is like the attitude towards a coward who has been slapped on the face and not defended himself. Katlansky, the editor, the "adviser," Taler's competitor, spreads the word as much as he can. Crab is wrapped up with his own concerns (his affair with the impoverished aristocrat's daughter, they say, is nearly over), and he hasn't been in the press for a number of days. Applebaum, the "meneger," who is responsible for the press and for getting the paper out, says as soon as Crab gets to *know* about it, he will not allow Eve to go on working on his premises. Bad for the reputation.

Eve has been to her brother's place only once, and even then in secret. They were ashamed for the quiet, modest, dignified neighborhood in which they were living. Their landlord—the author, the half-Rabbi and the father of married and unmarried daughters. The poor wretch is paying a very heavy price for her moments of pleasure. Her brother has already made mention of the "necessary operation" to her—in the proper way—but she trembled: She's afraid, she's afraid ... "Fool! Afterwards you'll go back to Russia, to our mother." Nothing more was needed. She fell to the ground and embraced his feet:

—Please don't write to mother about it, Shemaiale ... please don't tell her anything ... don't tell mother ... mother ...

The horror of her situation rose before her like a living thing in the shape of a short communication to her mother...

But they wouldn't let her shout: they might hear downstairs...

xxiii

I will record the matter as it happened.

It was Thursday—the day when Crab's weekly appears. Taler was sitting in his place, freely translating from the English a detailed review of the novel *Jungle*, which had caused a stir. Menuhin sat opposite, looking at the last galley proofs in front of him. The other "members of the editorial" sat at their various tasks. Suddenly Mr. Crab approached Taler in a strange floating, gliding manner, and scattered in front of him a cluster of unconnected remarks:

He should kindly tell his sister . . . no more . . . I have given Mr. Herry instructions . . . the caretaker . . . not to let her . . . I'm very sorry . . . pity . . . I don't know who is to blame . . . but my good name and the good name of my press . . . a pregnant girl . . .

Katlansky shifted on his seat in triumph. He could see in his enemy—in Taler—what he had never expected in his wildest dreams. Taler's answer came in whispers, so that it was swallowed up unheard above the noise and clatter of the wheels. But suddenly there was a lull in the commotion. Without standing up, Abraham Menuhin pushed the galley proofs aside and turned to Crab:

—I have something to say to you, Mr. Crab!

"Mr. Crab?"—The boss was amazed for a few moments— And what is it?

—It is . . . I would prefer to tell you in private.

Secrets? I have no secrets . . . no secrets . . .

Everyone was aware that the boss had meant to add "with you"—but he didn't.

Menuhin laughs characteristically. No secrets? Perhaps there are. We know, for example, all of us the secret of the prizes, which he, Mr. Crab, promises to pay to those who solve the riddles in the weekly. The competitors send postage stamps, as requested, with their replies. That amounts to a tidy sum. And Mr. Crab then announces that he has sent the prizes to someone or other in Hamburg or in Spain—and who can deny it? That and other tidbits, secrets . . .

What?!—Crab couldn't believe his ears. But he didn't leave his place and his glance wandered.

Menuhin continued.—But all this has nothing to do with anyone. Nor are we concerned with community secrets. But Mr. Crab should not be over-righteous! If he is unwilling to have this said to him in private—it has to be stated publicly . . . better not be too righteous . . . if there were *real men* here, all of them as one man would turn their backs on him the moment he drives a woman who is more innocent and better than himself off his premises.

—Has my sister appointed you her guardian?—Taler interrupted the speaker.

All work in the press had automatically come to a halt. Everyone sensed what was going to happen; they gathered round and stood in a circle.

That bright spark is taking the matter too much to heart—some of the workers whispered—Perhaps he's the one who did the damage, and not the "gentile."

—Bet you he was a partner—others conjectured.

—One eye on the grave, and the other . . .

—He's got his wits about him! . . . Applebaum remarked.

—Where are you off to?—Menuhin meanwhile exclaimed to his boss, seeing the latter about to escape his embarrassing situation ("as they say—mad"—Jacobson commented when explaining Crab's strange behavior during this episode)—don't worry about the good name of your press, and the good name of your papers. Its reputation, if I may say so, is not so great in any case. "You don't know who's to blame"—it's a lie! You know . . . everyone knows . . . there he stands . . ."

And Menuhin indicated Shtaktorov. And then occurred the sudden, unexpected scene. Shtaktorov—in his blue shirt—went pale (for the first time since the affair became known), got up and snatched from Jacobson the hammer which he was holding to straighten the page of print, with the intention of bringing it down on the Jew-boy's head. But the Jew-boy took hold of him by the hand and looked him straight in the eye:

Shtaktorka—Mirabeau—don't you remember your hat being changed . . . I have never hurt you . . .

There are moving scenes in a man's life.

xxiv

Maisey the innkeeper has a deep understanding of the human heart. "Lieberman is up for grabs!" he says. By "up for grabs" Maisey means a bachelor who has made up his mind to get married—come what may. Maisey recognizes at once, without being told, who is "up for grabs" and who isn't. There is no escape from it—Maisey says—Today it's you—tomorrow it's him. Sooner or later—there's no escape from it. Look, today I hear some young man saying: Who? Me? I should put my neck in a yoke? God forbid! Don't I see what success my friends have had who leaped before they looked? All, apparently, quite sound . . . and tomorrow . . . see, he's up for grabs himself!" "I have seen this, too," namely he, Maisey has seen it: "when a young man is *really* up for grabs, he is not too particular whether he's his chosen one's first or not. In short, gentlemen, Lieberman's "up for grabs"!

And Lieberman himself is, indeed, pulled in two directions. One direction: to take the little money he still has and go to the land of Israel, "even though he is a Territorialist in principle"; the second direction: to take the job which has been offered him in Amerson's press, and to go on living in this very dwelling where Menuhin lives, and where that girl whose sweetheart has gone to Oxford, makes the beds...

—It's marvelous, he sometimes says to Menuhin, to you, Abraham, I reveal everything, everything which is hidden and concealed within me; with you I speak with complete frankness; from you, Abraham, I conceal nothing ... I will tell you the truth ... I'm not an old bachelor ... but the time has come ... I'm not ugly, so it seems, but I don't appeal all that much to the girls I meet ... perhaps you know why? ...

—You need ... to find a mother ... you need a child to cuddle, who will pull your moustache ... who will thaw you out ... who will dispel your melancholy ... well, a pure, little foot ... well, simple ... do you hear?

—I will tell you the truth ...—Shalom Lieberman continues to confess to Abraham—my natural inclination developed very early ... and for some years since, I am afraid to say, I was seventeen, I have been carrying in my bosom a fantasy to meet some poor lame girl—I don't want a hunchback, I don't like hunchbacks—but to meet a poor lame girl and become attached to her—In moments of depression I imagine to myself, how she too rejects me ... pain ... great sorrow ... or sometimes I dream of taking some woman out of a bawdy house and marrying her ... how does it seem to you, father Abraham? ...

—You are not sure of yourself, my child—Menuhin shakes his head—and that's bad ...

—Bad, you say?—Lieberman is disturbed—that's it, that's it ... that's what I thought ... and so there only remains for me now ... there only remains for me now the other way: to go away from here ... to go, to go ... to flee ...

—To Palestine ...

—To America, to Palestine—to wherever my eyes carry me ...

—There's no need. I'm not good at giving advice, and I'm not a good guide. But, Shalom, so it seems to me: there's no need, there's no need simply to wander round from place to place. What will you do there? Palestine, land work—a good thing—when a man works the land he's not a caricature ... all other types of work ... well, however it is, you, Shalom, are *not* a land worker ... and in a press it's better for you to work here ... stay ... you have a little money ... I have something else in mind ...

xxv

The ten days of penitence.

In the Jewish quarter most of the commotion is a leftover from earlier times; there is no longer any soul in it—no longer ...

Abraham is looking for work—and there isn't any. He doesn't know English, and the English presses don't accept Jews even if they know the language. As for the Jewish presses—they have already heard about him, and not to his credit ...

Off the record, he has become a porter. He's strong.—

On leaving his employment with Crab, his social mission has finished, his sacrifice for the truth ... now he intends to put other things right ...

For some reason Jacobson has begun to frequent our house. He is nearly forty and married with children, and yet he still has a good nose for sniffing out a willing female.

Yesterday, the fast of Gedaliah, when Abraham returned from his day's work at nine o'clock in the evening, he found the young lady of the house taking her "mantle" from the broken wardrobe.

Menuhin fixed his tired eyes on her and deliberately engaged her in conversation—it's autumn outside ... not good for going out ...

—Mr. Jacobson says ...

—Jacobson's a liar ... Menuhin exclaimed openly, and with uncharacteristic coarseness—there is another girl already folding the papers in the press ... for some time now ... so you are invited for nothing, my friend ... what's the young lady's name? Betty ... No need to put a healthy head in a sick-bed, Betty ...

The girl Betty doesn't like the "angry bear" (in actual fact, Abraham resembles a lion more than a bear, and there is no anger in him!), but she is afraid of him, and she is particularly afraid of his powerful influence on Lieberman ...

—If the young lady Betty really wants to work—Abraham continued—he can be of some assistance to her. In the "kitchen" where we eat, they want a waitress. Maisey's wife is due to give birth soon. Have no fear ... in that "kitchen"—every customer is one of us. No harm will come to anyone there. That "kitchen" is not like any other "kitchen." People aren't even allowed to play cards there.

At this point the mother comes in complaining.

Excuse me, excuse me, Mr. Menuhin ... Is this "Our father, Abraham"! ...

She had never expected that he would advise her daughter to become a waitress ... They haven't fallen that far ... and Mr. Lieberman is listening, and he sits dumb ... "Oh Mr. Lieberman?"—

xxvi

There's no fathoming the mind of a pregnant woman; her ways are devious and strange. For a whole week Eve has vanished—and nobody knows where she's gone to. She is swallowed up in the great city, among the six millions—and there's no sign of her. She has not been to the girlfriend, with whom she lived until her condition became known. Abraham went to her brother's place to inquire about her, and was informed, if not explicitly, by Hayyah-Rachel that they really wanted to take her in, but on condition that she stop being stubborn, and agree to the advice of experienced women, to the advice of people interested in her welfare ... She had gone away in despair ... She had gone to Shtaktorov ... to tell him that her brother was going to sue him ... but Shtaktorov was in no state to listen to her—his real Russian essence has flared up sharply, and he is rolling round his room drunk the whole time.—

I can imagine—Lieberman is excited—I can imagine what hardship she has suffered this week ... and I can also imagine what an effort it cost our Abraham to go to Taler's place ... he hasn't been there for six months ... he didn't want to meet him ... Don't you know anything about it? Oh, it's a story in itself ... Taler's wife ... I gather ... loved him to distraction in her youth ... Abraham is worthy of being loved like that ... Eve, too, I gather, fled our group only because of him ... sometimes she cannot bear the look in his eyes ... sometimes ... in his presence she feels herself a sinner, although he ... he behaves towards her as only he can behave, and all the time he says: Never mind, Eve, never mind ... everything will be all right ... everything ... but she is foolish ... oh, foolish, foolish ... (a deep sigh).

The "fool"—is now living in our place. Abraham traced her to the house of a "good woman," and his discovery of her came about by means of Betty and her mother. He told mother and daughter the whole story: he added, that's how women are lost because of their imagined disgrace, their silly fear; he explained how he was frightened that in despair she might follow the advice she had been given, that was really bad, abhorrent, unnatural; he indicated, that everything could still be altered for the better, that the girl could still find the man to love her, and find shelter in happiness. The mother and daughter listened trembling; they thought that the whole conversation was revolving round their affair, and they were interested. From intense interest they agreed to be of help, even after they grasped the fact that it was not fictitious, and that Abraham was concerned with a real girl, and not a parable about them. Abraham took from Lieberman everything he had in his pocket. From it he gave a sum of money to the "good woman" for her hospitality, for her good intentions, and so that she wouldn't have any "demands" (she had already gone to the trouble of taking Eve to an expert on the subject, but the latter had said, that it was already too late . . .); the mother and daughter also took payment for their trouble.— Now the four of us sleep in one room. Happiness and heat.

Eve's pregnancy becomes more obvious from day to day—and her nerves are getting on top of her. To make a little more space in the room, they decided to remove the broken wardrobe to their own room—the mother and daughter's room. Abraham took hold of it and moved it with one hand. Betty, too, took hold of the wardrobe, which gave her an opportunity to show herself a little to the men and cried: Oh, how frightened I am . . . modder . . . but Eve for some reason was really frightened of the wardrobe, she turned white as chalk and leaned on Lieberman's shoulder . . . to what extent a pregnant woman's fears sometimes go!

Fear and . . . and embarrassment. The mother and daughter never once pass by their neighbor without expressing open contempt. Their "rival" in herself counts virtually for nothing. Betty isn't pregnant, and she is pregnant by a gentile ... and the child is in her womb ... and there are boils on her face ... "Never mind, Eve!—Abraham tells her as he goes to work—stay in the house ... do you know what I dreamed last night? I saw your elder brother in a dream ... you don't remember him ... you can well be proud of him, my daughter ... he died next to me in a tent in Siberia ... before he died he mentioned your name to me ... he loved you ... not your brother, but you—he loved ...

xxvii

Winter again. Evening classes and public lectures begin.

Even Mrs. Taler is fed up, apparently, with staying at home, and tomorrow she is making a public appearance in "Toynbee Hall" and will lecture on "The women's liberation movement in England."

Lieberman is working at Amerson's: he is earning quite well. His spirit is beginning to calm down under Abraham's merciful motherly hand. Abraham and Eve visit him in the evenings in his new lodgings. The rest of our colony—Abraham, Eve and I—have moved to Maisey's, to the top room in his "kitchen." We left our previous abode in disgrace. It was known through the courtyard that a pregnant woman was living with the "Russians," that the girl was pregnant by a gentile and that one of them—the best off—was going to marry her.

I cannot abide things like that—the old woman informed her neighbors—have you ever heard the like? ... A shame and a disgrace ... Isn't it? I've got a daughter ... my daughter says: "Modder, it's more than I can bear; show them the door; they are not men at all ..."

One of the neighbors remarks:

I saw one of them coming out of the missionaries' reading room...

Alas!—the landlady groaned—my daughter! do you hear that? Now I understand... everything's clear now...

But everything in fact—is still not clear. Lieberman is wondering and hesitant. At times—he complains—she is so repugnant to him!... he loves her, he hasn't stopped loving her... but... when he remembers, when he remembers...

—I know, Shalom, I know—Menuhin consoles him—it's hard for you... it seems to you a kind of blemish on her but, the main thing is... don't deceive yourself, Shalom, don't deceive yourself... you need her, and she needs you... and the main difficulty is that people will say... forgive me... people will say... well, you can well imagine what those base creatures will say... someone else took the choice part and left the remains to Lieberman... well, because of that, because of base creatures like them, will you ruin your life and hers?

—I can't forget him... I can't... him... the uncircumcised... at times Lieberman groans with the burden of his grief.

—Who? You?... what can you do?... What can you do? ... You, too, will forget him... by virtue of his child you will forget him... he will be a fine child, strong, healthy, lovely ... you see, Shalom, it sometimes seems so simple even to you ... it's only when you see her that the bitter thoughts arise ... but remember: when you think about it alone—then you will find it all so understandable... so simple.

—Oi,—Lieberman is impressed—it's true, it's true ... Whenever I'm away from her—I'm surprised at myself... I'm surprised how difficult it is for me... Oi, Abraham! How do you know all this?

And Abraham continues:

—It needs a little self-discipline, a little self-discipline, a little magnanimity, a little magnanimity... from one's baser nature to one's higher nature ... from the lower level to the upper level ...

—I, well, I ... Lieberman stammers—but she ... she ...

—She has already forgotten him, Shalom, she has already forgotten him, I tell you ... His memory is erased from her heart, erased ... She is not like the one you thought to go after ... she is a mother, simply a mother ... Whatever she did was not done deliberately ... It was the mother in her that pushed her into it ... and he ... he was an instrument in the hands of blind nature ... only an instrument, a tool ... and so Shalom, son of man, be a man ... it will all run its course ... for the time being she is living with me ... and when the day comes ... she will go to hospital, she will give birth, she will get better—and come to you, she and the child. Why don't you forget that bull? There will be no memory of him ... she hasn't mentioned him for a long time.

And Eve does not, indeed, mention Shtaktorov at all, neither for good nor for bad. Has she really forgotten him?—Who can tell? But she doesn't mention him, as though he had no place in her world. It may be that her silliness, which has now descended upon her through physical weakness and the weight of her body, is responsible ... Apathy! Overall, her face has become foolish-looking, and it has lost its vitality and grace ... my heart goes out to Lieberman ... and to Menuhin ... How hard it is for them both!

—Does Lieberman remember how he gave me the "Kreutzer Sonata," does he remember—Eve repeats this isolated remark over and over again, as though her empty heart can beget no other remark, and as though her whole salvation depends upon it.

In her heart of hearts she waits for happiness—everyone waits for happiness in his heart of hearts—but outwardly she declares that she does not believe that Lieberman will really take her under his wing. In all innocence she declares: Jacobson

met her and offered to care for her ... People imagine that once a person has fallen—everyone has the right to take advantage ... except that "our father Abraham" is her protector ... they are afraid of him ...
—And what will you do with the child, Eve?
—The child? ... I shall advertise in the newspapers ... perhaps good people will take him ... I have no way of supporting him ... I shall scarcely be able to support myself ...
Her stomach is like a crescent moon—and she is not fit to take on any job now to earn her living. Her stomach is like a crescent moon, and she doesn't carry it with the pride of a married woman, but neither does she make any overt efforts to conceal it. Our free society influences her too—simple and "unsophisticated" as she is—so as not to be too ashamed of her pregnancy. Abraham's hypnotic suggestion that the embryo in her womb is an important fact, of great significance, a lovely thing, is beyond the understanding of the clientele of Maisey's kitchen and outside it. And Abraham does even more. He does not resort to the method of silence, namely to pass in deliberate silence over what should, so to speak, be laughed at, that there is an imagined shame in it. No, not even imagined shame, but rather honor, boundless honor and joy. At every favorable moment he strokes her hair and says:
—Now, my Eve, how much longer ... when will you make us glad with the blessed fruit of your womb ... You have seen Maisey's little one, haven't you? ... You will have a little one like that too ... you will suckle him, you will carry him in your arms ... you will learn, you will learn ... you will bring him up to do good deeds ... and your Shalom will see it with his own eyes ... when, Eve, when will there be this sign?

xxviii

The book of Genesis states: "And the man gave names to the animals and beasts." From which we learn that it is in the nature of man to call everything by its proper name. And Abraham Menuhin—is a *man*.

Mrs. Taler's lecture in Toynbee Hall, which was not delivered, in spite of the large audience present and then the lecturer's arrival at the appointed hour—was not delivered because of Menuhin.

I had not previously known that side of him: his capacity to create scandals!

Hayyah-Rachel was adorned in a little bonnet with two edges curving downwards, not unlike the bonnets worn by ladies of the Salvation Army, and decked out with flowers and feathers. For the occasion she combined emancipation, enlightenment and understanding with due regard to feminine apparel and grace. "People used to think—she simpered to her listeners before going to the platform—that a progressive woman had to be ugly, ponderous, a 'blue stocking'. Thank God, those times have passed!"

But as the speaker was ascending the platform, accompanied by Mr. Taler in the role of chairman, *he* approached them and said quietly: Cannot the honorable lecturers pay any heed to doing something for their own flesh and blood, who is soon to become a mother, and who has no place to rest her head?

—Oh, good evening ... Menuhin ...

Menuhin was covered all over with the flour he had been carrying just previously. The dolled-up woman moved her skirts aside to avoid dirtying them, and said: It is very kind of Mr. Menuhin to come to hear the lecture. Old friends always remain friends ...

—The lecture? He hadn't come to listen to lectures. Hadn't they heard his question ...

—Would it not be better for Mr. Menuhin—the couple evaded him with a movement of dissatisfaction ... to come to our home ... as he did once ... this is not the time ... as he could see ... and anyway, whatever was possible would be done ... in spite of everything, in spite of his threats and his group of friends ... Shtaktorov would be summoned to court ... it was dangerous to summon him. Shtaktorov was capable of plunging a knife into his enemy's body ... but he would be summoned ...

Good ... Menuhin retorted—summon him ... but what has a summons to do with this? ... What help will a summons be?

Christianity!—the lecturer could not contain herself—don't take anyone to court ... "turn the other cheek" ... "don't judge and don't be judged" ... Oh, that's why Mr. Menuhin doesn't want to listen to my lecture ... the modern Christians for some reason all object to women's liberation ...

Not women's liberation, Mrs. Taler—Abraham Menuhin shouted—not women's liberation—the objection is—to whores and whoredom ...

Yes, to whores and whoredom—Abraham raised his voice—not to freedom, not to liberation ... liberation ... what liberation? Liberation from what, and why liberation for old whores ... old, even if they are thirty ... whores—even if Mr. Taler accompanies them ...

xxix

★ ★ ★

xxx

Two more months have passed. Everything is finished, everything.

* * *

And after everything is finished—everlasting distress, everlasting distress.

xxxi

* * *

xxxii

"And that's how it is, that's it," as he used to say, *him*. I can't hold out any more. I can't hold out any more.

Without my having noticed it—I shall soon have been here two full years. The world and its fullness. I can't hold out any more.

My illness drains me, overcomes me. It has caught my chest. It gnaws at my lung. This is real essence. That is the only truth.

I have become even more irritable and less just towards myself and others. Justice! Justice! To hell with it! ...

Only one thing is certain now. My poor existence will soon cease to be, soon ... my situation worsens from minute to minute—it is no longer sufferable ... yet I will suffer it ... and my life will end. Not in beauty and not in the fullness of age ... beauty—what is beauty? Beauty is for art ... Fullness of days—oh, fullness of days ...

And he, Abraham Menuhin ... the life of Abraham Menuhin ... I don't know all that life ... but what was it ... a fraud, a fraud ... hardship without cease ... unwanted sorrow ... and even if there were a few sparks—what did they come to? What could they have come to? Decay and nothingness ... a twinkling of the eye—and darkness forever.

Man is good, man is evil—it's a lie, a lie! Man is not good and man is not evil ... there is only man's oppression, man's loss, man's distress ...

But no one listens to our voice. Our voice is unheard.

The verdict is returned.

xxxiii

Shtaktorov was deported to his native land by court order—and left three persons behind: one sick woman writhing in pain, one baby in swaddling clothes, and one creature—as long as it survives.

What a terrible moment when the flashing blade of the kitchen knife pierced deep into the victim's head—a terrible moment.

Maisey's "kitchen" was terrified.

But the drunken beast was not satisfied with that: he wanted to plunge it into Menuhin's heart ...

Let them hand me over to the court, to hard labor ... why have you stolen what belongs to me? Give me back what's mine ... give me my little Jewess ... I'll swing for it ... give me back my Jewess ... I don't need her ... but don't take ... what is mine ... I'll kill!

The voice was a swine's grunting in the forest; the movements were flames breaking out of shavings. The disaster occurred three months ago.

Poor Lieberman. His mind did not become unhinged when "the revelation suddenly dawned upon him" that all the time he had fed himself on error, on error and through the guilt of "that man, that man."

Her relationship with Shtaktorov had not stopped for a single day, a single day. Had it not been the case, the gentile would not have been so brazen. Where would he have drawn such brazen strength to kill and destroy, were he not certain that she was his, that she was his, and that Menuhin was stealing her from him by his protection?

Menuhin, Menuhin—he has ruined his life, Lieberman's life. He had not let him travel to his goal, he had not let him do what he thought was right; he had duped him with deceit, he had taken away his last penny, until he no longer had the means to flee from his troubles. He had no means to move from there, to travel...

But he did, in the end, move away. Lieberman moved away, he went.

I, too, am going away.

xxxiv

Eve wept. Not, of course, for the first time. She is at her wits' end. The child is not well. She brought him from the hospital to Maisey's place almost naked—and he caught cold. And anyway she doesn't know what to do with him, she doesn't know how to handle him. A first-time mother needs a mother herself to look after her. The child will die, it will die.

But the child doesn't die. It has a wide nose, its father's nose, a coarse broad face...

A place has been found for her. A wet-nurse is required in that very house, in which Taler lives, for the Rabbi's married daughter. Taler and his wife, of course, declared that they would move their lodgings if Eve so much as dared to come there and shame them. But who pays any attention to them? But what's to be done with Jonathan, Jonathan the son of Fyodor Shtaktorov? Eve cannot be parted from him. Who can she leave him with?

xxxv

Abraham Menuhin is still alive! He came out of hospital sick, with a wound in his head—but he is alive. He leans on a stick, but there is hope that he may soon recover, and won't need it. The man is strong. His complexion has darkened. The color of his face is dark. His features now resemble the face of Jesus in the picture by Murillo. When he saw me, he said: "Ya, ya—Out of the depths."

xxxvi

Maisey's wife spread her palms and said in her broken voice: what can she do, what can she do? She can't take all the world's abandoned children into her house, feed them, nurse them, look after them. What do they expect of her? She can't take on the whole world's troubles...

Abraham implored her and said: Sarah is right, right. But we aren't going out looking for all the abandoned children in the world to gather them into our house. This little one is not just any abandoned child. He's one of us. He has no father. He belongs to us all. As long as we are here—the child must be here too.

Maisey heard what he said and after his fashion thought he detected a hint that if his wife didn't consent to let the *bastard* stay with her, we would leave his "kitchen"—and his wrath was kindled, and he let it be known that we could weigh the favors we were doing him in general and the fact that we were lodging with him in particular and stick them ... and there he stopped.

xxxvii

Eve disappeared again. That too could have been prophesied from the beginning. Sick and angry she went to become wet-nurse to a strange child. She promised to put aside three quarters of her wages for Mrs. Maisey for taking Jonathan—provided she didn't fail there and they didn't dismiss her from her charge. But she fled of her own accord. After all she was scarcely eighteen, and there in the "Reverend's" house they also expected her to do the cooking and the washing. And she couldn't do cooking and washing! And they hadn't laid that down originally! There's no justice in the world! She couldn't stay there any longer!

Eve, the mother, disappeared—without a trace. Where could she have gone? To her mother in Russia?—Where could she have got the fare? No, a more likely guess is that some obliging folk arranged transport for her to the capital of the Argentine. There's a great demand there for women's flesh.

xxxviii

I, the writer, am still here. The waters of the fountain have started to flow again.

The wheel goes round.

"The sum doesn't add up, the calculation has gone wrong"—but what's the point of calculations. Which of us is entitled to calculate? As long as the *soul* is in us—we give thanks...

The sum total of Abraham Menuhin's life is not great—I complained—but the individual numbers...

And there are still individual numbers, a few. And even if only one number—how sublime!

He is still alive, he is sick and alive; he is still alive.

I pray now—the man told me—for two things only, so that I may bless my existence. I need two miracles, one for me and one for Jonathan, and both of them in the negative. For myself—I haven't a shirt to my back, and I sleep in my overcoat in summer—may I not contract leprosy... and may I be spared from disease... but no. As long as Jonathan doesn't fall ill—I do not fear even that, provided only the child doesn't fall ill! Let not the child fall ill. I am certain that *he has his father's strength and his mother's brother's soul.* Let him not fall ill. I cover him in his mother's brother's coat. Let there be a miracle. Let him grow.

All day the child is in his arms. "One baby movement from him—the happy father declares—makes all the troubles in the world worthwhile." Jonathan, the round infant with his lively eyes, his soft neck, his sprouting hair, his frail skull . . .

Last year's summer brought us another revelation.

The saplings in Springfields, the distant garden in the north of the city, are small, but the square is nice. It is closed at eight o'clock in the evening—and we are really sorry about that. From too much walking we have got blisters on our toes—and it's hard going back.

At night our places in Maisey's house are let to others, people who pay, but the nights are warm—and Menuhin and I stroll about Commercial Street, and see all our contemporaries there, who spend the nights walking. They are many . . .

The Final Scroll

THE WORD OF ABRAHAM came to me in Springfields before the garden was closed behind us, saying:

You ask me whether I think about death, and what I think about death? I am not far off death—and I think about it, but what can I think about it, when death itself wipes out all thinking about it?

I shall surely die this winter time, one icy night. I shall lay me down out of the policeman's sight, near a fence—and my soul will depart in purity. The last pang will be in me, and the fine snow and my childhood memories will lull me to sleep until I expire. My memories of childhood are of a life of hardship, but at that moment of eternity the best of them will emerge to accompany me. I count on it.

My parents were penniless, and I studied in the Talmud Torah in the women's gallery of the "cold synagogue." Poor beggars lodged there, in that same women's gallery, they and their wives and children. It was a Friday, the eve of Sabbath, the burden of Torah study weighs heavy only until noon—I am in good spirits. Then I saw in the corner a sallow face—a woman weeping. "Woman! woman! good woman! why are you crying? Are you hungry? Come and we will go to my home. I am going for our meal. We've got cooked marrows today. My mother will give you half my share." And the woman went with me ... I was six years old at the time.

"And the man they found was about forty,"—Spinner the "news editor" in Crab's newspapers will write and pass the news on to Taler so that he can shorten the style and take out the superfluous words—"apart from the child in his arms he had nothing."

I will be dead asleep then in the darkness, and there will be nobody to continue in the proofs: "The child was clasped to the dead man, sleeping a child's sweet sleep."

—And this addition is needed. The child who will be left an orphan *after me*, the child who will not come under the rod of teachers and educators, the child whom I carried in my arms, whom I gave milk to drink, who was clasped to me in the most final moments of my fleeting existence, who was sleeping a child's sweet sleep in my arms—he will grow ...

Thus he spoke to me in the Springfields garden, before the sun went down, Abraham the typesetter—the proof-reader—the porter—the father.

And the sun went down: it went down in rich red grease and set. The little trees were silent. The keeper closed the park.

About the Book and Translator

By the time Joseph Chaim Brenner arrived in London (where *Out of the Depths* was written) in 1904, his literary reputation was already established by a volume of short stories and a previous novel, *In Winter*. Born in Russia in 1881, Brenner at the age of twenty-four had fled the disorders of the Russian Empire for the mean peace of London's East End.

Out of the Depths is concerned with a group of Russian immigrants in London who work for a Jewish daily newspaper. They are caught up in a conflict with the owner when he seeks to introduce a typesetting machine into the newspaper shop. Following an unsuccessful strike, the impoverished workers decline into a general collective misery that is relieved only by the strength and honesty of the central character.

The language of *Out of the Depths* has a remarkably modern energy. Brenner anticipates literary techniques that came into wide use only later. The employment of stream of consciousness, shifting perspectives, and emotive presentation and the use of vocabulary from the Yiddish, Russian, German, and English languages have a startling impact, a texture that Dr. Patterson faithfully captures while conforming to the demands of English idiom.

Employing an ancient language in a modern idiomatic style, this little-known work by a writer of remarkable honesty gives intense expression to the social upheavals of the time and to the profound moral questioning that for some was almost a consequence of living in the first years of this century.

David Patterson's translation of *Out of the Depths* received the Webber Prize for translation in 1989.

David Patterson is president of the Oxford Centre for Postgraduate Hebrew Studies.